Merry Blissmas

Merry Blissmas

Biker Bitches, #3

Jamie Begley

Young Ink Press Publication
YoungInkPress.com

Copyright © 2015 by Jamie Begley

Edited by C&D Editing and Hot Tree Editing
Cover Art by Young Ink Press

All rights reserved.

No part of this book may be reproduced in any form or by any electronic or mechanical means including information storage and retrieval systems, without permission in writing from the author. The only exception is by a reviewer, who may quote short excerpts in a review.

This book is a work of fiction. Names, characters, places, and incidents either are products of the author's imagination or are used fictitiously. Any resemblance to actual persons, living or dead, events, or locales is entirely coincidental.

This work of fiction is intended for mature audiences only. All sexually active characters portrayed in this ebook are eighteen years of age or older. Please do not buy if strong sexual situations, rape, violence, drugs, and explicit language offends you.

ISBN: 069260572X
ISBN 13: 9780692605721

Connect with Jamie,
JamieBegley@ymail.com
www.facebook.com/AuthorJamieBegley
www.JamieBegley.net

Chapter One

"Do you think Willa would like this one?"

Bliss looked up from the mound of scarves on the display table to the one Ginny was holding up. The pale colors and pretty pattern would suit Willa, but the scarf was lame. Bliss didn't voice her opinion, however. Instead, she said, "She'll love it."

Bliss hated scarves unless they were tied around her wrists. The thought had her turning from the table to cross to the one with the Christmas jewelry display, the fake stones glistening under the store lighting. One in particular with glittering reds and golds caught her eye. It was a golden Christmas tree pendant with shining red ornaments.

Christmas was coming earlier every year. It wasn't even Halloween yet, and stores wanted everyone to start their holiday shopping.

It wouldn't be long before the women at the clubhouse put up the Christmas tree. As soon as Halloween was over, Raci would make the men drag the artificial tree out of the attic. Rider would steal kisses as he helped decorate. Train would hang back and do what no one else wanted to do, storing all the boxes away when they were done. Viper and Winter would laugh and tell them they were over decorating the tree. The other members would fuss about it going up so early then move into the kitchen and make apple cider punch, which they would drink. Then the decorating party would become a fuck-fest that would take them a couple of days to recover from.

Bliss blinked back the water that had formed in her eyes. Crying had never done her any good, and she certainly wasn't going to shed tears in public. That lesson had been deeply ingrained in her before she knew how to talk.

As a child, whenever she cried, it was quietly and efficiently dealt with by her mother. A child's loud cries or screams could get them thrown out of whichever homeless shelter they had found for the night. Left with three mouths to feed after their father had died from a heroin overdose, her mother couldn't afford to keep a roof over their heads and went from one shelter to the next. Whatever money she could scrounge together went to feed her own heroin addiction instead of making sure her children had a safe bed to sleep in each night.

She was good at pretending to be clean around others, but her mother didn't keep the pretense up in front of her children. Child and Family Services stepped in, removing her brothers when she was four, telling her crying mother they needed school and she couldn't financially care for three children anyway. They promised, as soon as she was back on her feet, she could try for custody again. It never happened. Most of her money went to the drug she shot through her veins, and what was left went to providing them with what food or clothes they needed.

To her dying day, Bliss would remember the sight of her blond-haired, green-eyed brothers, both of them fighting against the workers taking them away from their sister. Neither had cared about their mother, but they had been the ones caring for her, and as a result, they hadn't wanted to let her go.

Her lips tightened. Brand and Stone were the only ones who had ever loved her, and she had lost them, just as she had lost Shade. Everyone she loved had been taken away from her. She should've been used to it, but with each loss, it became harder to remember what it felt like to actually be happy. She became more bitter and felt as if her heart had been packed in ice.

Her thumb brushed over the small necklace. Before she had been thrown out of The Last Riders motorcycle club, she would have pouted until Train, Rider, or Crash bought it for her, even though she could easily afford it herself. Viper, the club president, made sure each of the members could afford whatever they wanted.

Bliss had a hefty amount of money in her savings account, which she refused to touch. When she was old and men no longer wanted her, she would be able to care for herself, unlike her own mother who had made herself available to any man with enough money to support her drug habit.

By the time she was fifteen, her mother had become a club whore for the Devil's Rejects. When her mother hadn't returned home for two weeks, she had been thrown out of the tiny room her mother rented at a hotel, and Bliss had to track her down at the clubhouse.

Once there, her mother refused to leave. Stark, the club president, promised her a back room to sleep in at night. He swore to keep the men away from her. She should have known better.

Stark raped her the first night she spent in the clubhouse.

The following morning, she managed to dress herself and beg her mother to leave. However, her pleas fell on deaf ears, and Stark dragged her back to her room, threatening to kill both of them if she tried to leave. Young and terrified, she stayed.

When she had just turned seventeen, her mother became ill. The bikers were going to throw her mom away, since no one wanted an ill junkie and she no longer served her purpose. Her mom would have ended up in a state-run facility. Bliss held a part-time job at the time, handing the money over to Stark each payday, but she didn't make enough to support both of them if they left, especially with all the medical needs her mother had. Stark gave her another option. She could earn her and her mother's keep by replacing her as one of the club whores.

Bliss could have run away from it all, and to that day, she didn't know why she hadn't. She certainly had no love lost between her and her mother, but she had been all Bliss had left in the world. She didn't even have a high school diploma. She and her mother had moved so often, Child and Family Services had lost track of her long before.

Although her mother was a worthless piece of shit, something was better than nothing. Therefore, she became the club whore, letting the men use her, all the while burying the disgust for herself deep within until she no longer felt anything when she was under their thrusting bodies.

As she grew older, she realized Stark would have never let her go. He had only pretended to give her the option so she would be more compliant when his men took her. A whore was no fun if they had to constantly rape her to take what they wanted. No, they wanted her on her knees, willingly giving them the blow jobs they demanded.

Despite Stark letting his men fuck her, he made sure they knew she was his old lady. Being the meanest and roughest of all the bikers, she had dreaded when he took her. Each time became worse than the one before, often leaving her bruised and hurting. He would make himself come when he was fucking her by strangling her until she passed out. Each time she lost consciousness she thought it would be the last, that death would finally claim her.

She began thinking about leaving the club when her mother died. With no reason to tolerate them or their abuse anymore,

Bliss had made plans, becoming more and more frightened of Stark's violent behavior.

The night she was rescued from the Devil's Rejects was one she would never forget. By the time daylight hit Ohio, she was at The Last Riders' clubhouse, and the last vestiges of gentleness and kindness in her disposition were gone. She quit being a sucker and thinking things were going to get better in her life. They weren't. Men were all the same, wanting the same thing—to use her and not feel guilty for it.

After the Devil's Rejects, it took her a while to recognize that The Last Riders were different. They had the same goal of rocking their nuts off in her, but at least they didn't hurt her or make her feel like a whore. They even allowed her to try to become a member when she asked.

Cash and Shade had warned her that the brothers would treat her fairly, but they wouldn't tolerate the women being catty to one another. However, she had ignored the rules, becoming immune to their threats of throwing her out of the club.

She had thrown herself at the male members who were married right in front of their wives. The worst had been when she had insinuated that she would have sex with Lucky when he had only wanted to talk to her privately. That had been the final straw, but the sad part was she had been striking out to hurt them as much as she was hurting.

She should have backed away from Shade the night The Last Riders' enforcer had become drunk enough to expose his feelings for Lily. The innocent woman hadn't even known of Shade's interest in her.

She had stolen his heart without even trying, and while Bliss had used every weapon at her disposal to turn his attention to her, she didn't have long black hair and violet eyes. Her own short, spiky, blonde hair was the exact opposite, her eyes a dull blue.

Then there was Lily's sweet innocence, which was in direct contrast to the sex games Bliss excelled in and had come to enjoy. Furthermore, Lily ran from being a submissive, whereas Bliss embraced it.

The Dom/sub relationship made her feel cared for and loved during the short time she had managed to capture Shade's attention. Then she not only couldn't capture his attention, but she rarely managed to catch a glimpse of him.

"Do you think Kelly would like this?" A young male voice drew Bliss's attention from the necklace in her hand and the memories in her mind to the man standing at the jewelry counter a few feet away.

Bliss recognized the father and son duo from the high school football games she had attended with The Last Riders. Jace, who had been the star quarterback for Treepoint High the previous year, was a younger version of the man who indulgently waited for his son to pick a present. His father, Drake Hall, was the local realtor whose loud yells from the stands had made his presence known to her and everyone around him.

She also recognized the young man standing next to him, Cal. He had also played on the football team as defense, and Drake had yelled just as loudly for him during the games. Bliss remembered Rachel, Drake's cousin, telling the women in the club one night at dinner that Drake had become Cal's guardian when Cal's father had been arrested for helping Lily and Beth's father kidnap them and Razer. All the women had been upset when they had learned Cal's baby sister had been put in foster care.

Bliss watched Drake from under her lashes. It was hard not to. His hard, sensual looks would make any woman take a second glance, but the body that went with them was enough to make her lick her lips. He was tall, muscular, and his biceps stretched his shirt tightly. She had to admit she was a sucker for a good set of biceps.

Bliss had caught him staring at her more than a few times in the past. If it weren't for the rules of The Last Riders that forbade her from having sex beyond club members, she would have approached him eagerly. Instead, she had ignored his lingering gaze. However, Bliss reminded herself she was no longer held back by any of the rules the club imposed. She could do whatever she wanted.

Sauntering closer, she caught a glimpse of the heart necklace dangling from Jace's fingertips.

"Depends on what you want to tell her," Bliss cut in to the men's conversation. "If you want to tell her she's your one and only, buy it. If you want to keep her guessing, pick something else."

"Like what?" Jace's curiosity was immediately caught.

Bliss's fingertip tapped the glass display case, pointing to a popcorn necklace with two dangling pearls.

"That's cool." Jace motioned to the saleswoman, who pulled the necklace out of the display case. "What do you think, Dad?"

"I think you should take her advice. She would know better than I would what a teenage girl would like."

"Cal?" Jace turned to his friend.

The other boy stared at it briefly. "Don't ask me. I think you should give her a gift card."

"That's why you don't have a girlfriend," Jace wisecracked.

Bliss was still tuned in to what Drake had said. She sincerely doubted she would know better than him; those lines of experience on his face showed he had broken more than his fair share of women's hearts. She noticed the interest in his eyes deepen at her silent perusal.

“Thanks for the help,” Jace said after telling the saleswoman he wanted to buy Bliss’s suggestion. “My name is Jace, and this is my dad, Drake Hall.”

A smile tugged at her lips when he held out his hand for her to shake. Bliss took it.

“Your girlfriend will love her gift.”

“It’s a make-up present. She found out I went out with another girl.”

“That should do it…for a first-time offense.”

Jace laughed. “What if I do it again? Buy her the heart necklace?”

Bliss’s gaze narrowed on him. *Yeah, like father like son.*

“No, buy her your favorite shade of lipstick so she can give you something to remember her by when she kisses your ass good-bye.”

Jace and his friend moved to the side to pay for the necklace, his smile dying away with her sarcastic reply.

“That was a little harsh.” Drake’s amused voice drew her attention from his cocky son.

“Maybe you should have taught your son about loyalty and how to treat a woman when you were teaching him the ABCs.”

Drake gave her a wicked smile. “There are some things that are better for a man to figure out on his own.”

“I have a feeling Jace is a chip off the old block,” she stated.

Drake laughed, causing several of the customers to look at them curiously. “You do realize you’re getting angry about Jace cheating on a young woman you don’t even know when you just met him a few minutes ago.”

Bliss couldn’t even explain to herself why she was so angry. “No woman likes to hear about men cheating on their women.”

“You have a problem with men cheating? Belonging to The Last Riders, I thought cheating would be second nature to you.

Does it only make you angry when you're not the one they're cheating with?"

Bliss paled. "Actually, I didn't take you for a man who listened to gossip. For your information, none of the men who are married have cheated. Also for your information"—Bliss stood on her toes so the man towering over her could hear her better—"I don't belong to The Last Riders."

Chapter Two

Bliss turned on her booted heels, leaving him and his son staring after her. She stopped only long enough to tell Ginny she would meet her back at the house they were renting from Willa before she stormed from the department store.

She had known better than to let Ginny convince her to go shopping together to buy Willa a thank-you present for all she had done for them. Bliss had agreed only because it was the only way Willa would accept a thank-you from her. She still felt ashamed of herself for the way she had treated Willa when she had believed she and Shade had been together. Deep down, she had known she was wrong, that Shade would never cheat on Lily.

One by one, the men were falling for women outside the club, and it had been the final straw when Lucky had fallen in love and married Willa.

She had reacted out of anger and had hurt a woman who had turned the other cheek and offered her a home with Ginny, who worked for Willa at her bakery at the church. She rented a house to them that Willa no longer needed, since she had moved into the clubhouse with Lucky until he could build their new home beside the club. Willa had also hired Ginny to help out with the cooking at the clubhouse. *I would enjoy that if I still lived there,* she thought morosely.

Bliss ran her red-tipped fingernails through her short hair fastidiously when the wind blew it as she walked the short distance back to the house she and Ginny shared. She couldn't stand long hair. As soon as her hair reached a certain length on her nape, she would go to the salon and get it cut.

As she turned down a side street, the sound of motorcycle motors roared in the air.

With iron determination, she didn't turn to look. She forced herself to put one foot in front of the other as they rode past when what she wanted to do was run after them, jump on the back of one of the brothers' bikes, and snuggle against them. She didn't like being alone after growing used to being surrounded by the men and women of the club.

The silence when she entered her new abode was disheartening. At the clubhouse, there was always someone to talk or argue with, music blaring, and people laughing. She missed the laughter most of all.

Bliss went upstairs to the bedroom she had claimed before Ginny even had a chance. It had an adjoining private bathroom and the biggest closet.

She took off her jeans and sweatshirt, throwing them into the dirty clothes basket before gathering a clean pair of sweats and a T-shirt. She then showered meticulously. Even though she didn't have a clubhouse of men to keep happy any longer, she shaved all over before washing her hair twice, the feeling of the warm water soothing her. When the water ran cold, she climbed out to dry off and dress.

Leaving her short hair wet since it never took long to dry, she then went downstairs to make herself dinner. Ginny often volunteered to cook for the both of them, but Bliss was sick of shared meals and eating what someone else was in the mood for.

She pulled a cup of microwavable mac and cheese out of the cabinet and heated it up. Then, curling up on the couch, she flipped on the television and was contentedly eating when Ginny returned with several packages.

"I thought you were just going to buy Willa a thank-you gift."

"I was, but they had a clearance sale, and all my clothes are getting too small, so I stocked up on a few things I needed."

The young woman needed more than a few. She had three pairs of jeans and several T-shirts, and that was about it. It reminded Bliss of when she had been living on the streets and kept what few clothes she had in her backpack.

Ginny packed her bags upstairs then came back down.

"I was going to fix myself a hamburger, would you like one?"

"No, thanks. I already ate."

As Ginny's expression filled with hurt, Bliss kept her eyes on the television screen. She wasn't about to become BFFs with her new roommate. The young woman was obviously naïve and innocent, so they would have nothing in common, and truthfully, Bliss was tired of losing friends.

She was relieved when Ginny disappeared into the kitchen.

Her program was almost over when Ginny returned, carrying her plate of food.

Although the girl tried to engage in chitchat as she sat down to watch the program with her, Bliss gave only monosyllabic replies.

"I guess I'll go upstairs, put away my new clothes, and wrap Willa's present."

"Okay."

Ginny walked toward the steps then paused, coming back to stand beside the couch.

"Is there a reason you don't like me?"

Bliss gaped up at her. Women like Ginny never confronted someone when they weren't happy.

"I don't dislike you."

"You've made it very plain you don't want to be friends."

"Girls like you never want to be friends with women like me."

"What are you talking about?" A frown showed her confusion.

Bliss sighed. "I'm a bitch. I've tried to be friends with women like you, but I fail every time. I make them mad and hurt their feelings. I try to steal their men, which *really* makes them hate me. So, I'm just saving both of us the pain of living in the same house once you decide to hate my guts."

"You actually try to steal your friends' husbands?"

"All but one, and that was Evie's husband."

"Not that I know who Evie is, but why didn't you try to steal her husband?"

"If you knew Evie, you wouldn't have to ask that question. She would knock my teeth out. Her husband is King. He opened the new restaurant and bar in town."

"I haven't been in there yet. It's a little out of my budget," Ginny said wryly.

Bliss rolled her eyes. "I'm sure there are a couple of guys who would be more than willing to treat you."

"I don't need a man to pay my way when we go out."

"See, I told you I would make you mad."

"I'm not angry, I'm just stating a fact." Ginny stared at her curiously. "Do you only go to places like that when someone else is paying?"

"Of course." Bliss shrugged. "My money goes into a savings account. I'm not going into a nursing home that hires God knows who. I'll be able to afford my own caretaker."

"What if you don't get old? What if you get killed in an accident or drop dead suddenly?"

Bliss stared up at the woman, dumbfounded. "Morbid much?"

"I'm not the one saving for a personal caregiver."

Touché. "What *are* you saving for?"

"You have to earn more than you spend to save, and I'm still trying to make ends meet."

Bliss frowned. "I'm not trying to get personal, but Willa's not even charging us that much rent, and I'm splitting the bills with you. You have two jobs: one, helping Willa with her baking and the other, working part-time at The Last Riders' clubhouse, cooking. You should be doing more than making ends meet."

"I paid all the utility deposits, and Willa offered to sell me this house, so I want to come up with a deposit before she changes her mind or someone else buys it."

"Willa's not like that. If she offered to let you buy this house, she will."

"I don't want to take a chance. I would never get enough credit to purchase a home like this. Willa is willing to take less than market value because she and Lucky are building their own home. I want a place to call my own that no one can take away from me."

Bliss swallowed hard. Ginny sounded just like her when she was her age. She still remembered how naïve she had been. It had taken her a lot of years for the truth to finally smack her across the face.

There was no such thing as home. It was a fictional word to describe a house, just like the people who lived in them calling themselves a family. As soon as trouble hit their door, however, they were quick to throw in the towel and toss it all away, exactly like she had.

Every single time she had begun to believe she had a home when she was younger, she would come home from school to find her meager possessions sitting outside a padlocked door and her mother explaining they had to find a new place to stay. What followed were weeks at homeless shelters until she could make enough money to rent them another small place.

It became normal to see a stranger taking her mother in a dark alley or the backseat of their car while she would patiently wait for her in whatever fast food restaurant was closest. She would eat her small hamburger and fries slowly so she wouldn't get strange looks from people wondering why she was sitting by herself so long.

But she was older and wiser. She could find a place to sleep anywhere, but she would never put her belief in having the dream of a perfect home with a white picket fence.

Even being a member of The Last Riders hadn't prevented her from losing the room she had thought of as hers. She had been able to share her bed or one of the brothers' if she had wanted, but she had also had the option of closing the door and being left alone when she had wanted to curl up on her bed and watch television or read a book while knowing the other members would still be there when she opened the door.

She was on her own, though. Neither the men nor the women talked to her anymore. Bliss knew it was because of her own behavior, but it still fucking hurt. They could have stuck a knife in her stomach, and she would have remained loyal to them.

Her mom had always told her to obey the rules of whatever house they lived in, because it wasn't their home and they could be thrown out. Her mother had been right.

She had learned a lot of hard lessons in her life, but leaving The Last Riders had been the hardest of all.

Chapter Three

Bliss sat on the bleachers next to Ginny, surveying the large crowd. She had accepted Ginny's invitation to go to the basketball game in hope of seeing a few of The Last Riders. They loved sports and supported the school activities, thanks to Viper's wife, Winter, who was the principal of the local alternative school. She really left them no choice.

"I'm going to get some popcorn. Want some?"

"Yes, please." Ginny reached for her purse.

"My treat." Bliss stood, taking off down the long flight of steps then walking in front of the crowded bleachers to the concession stand. She felt several eyes on her as she went. Bliss knew it was the wives of The Last Riders' watching her.

She was glad she had taken extra care with her appearance that night. Her leather leggings clung to her ass, and the black jersey sweatshirt had silver studs that flashed as she walked past.

She breezed past Rider and Train, not giving them a second glance as she got in line behind Shade.

"I'll take a medium with two bottled waters." His deep voice brought an ache to her heart.

"No butter?" She took a step forward so he could hear her over the roars coming from inside the gym. "You love butter."

Shade turned his head, his cold blue gaze making her take a step back.

Turning back around, he paid then moved to the side to wait as the kid behind the counter rushed to fill his order.

"It's not for me, it's for Viper and Winter."

"Lily's not here with you tonight?"

"No, she's home with John. He has a cold."

Bliss paled at the reminder of Shade's child. It never failed to thrust a blade through her heart.

"I hope he feels better soon," she said sincerely.

"Do you?" He took the bag of popcorn and waters from the kid before turning to face her.

Bliss paled even more. "Of course. I wouldn't wish anything bad on your child, Shade."

Shade ran his eyes over her body critically.

Bliss had never been self-conscious, but she had noticed the dark circles under her eyes, and if she had seen them, Shade would. No detail, however small, ever got past him.

"You've lost weight."

"Shade, please—"

"Don't ask. You already know the answer."

"I'd do anything if you could talk Viper into letting me come back," Bliss pleaded.

"There's nothing I can do to convince Viper of that, and I don't want to. You pushed our friendship too far. Even when I kept telling you to stop being a bitch to the women, you kept pushing."

Bliss avoided his perceptive gaze, looking away and pretending she was interested in the basketball game. She noticed Drake Hall was in the gymnasium doorway, watching her and Shade instead of the game.

"Why couldn't you love me?" Bliss whispered to Shade's retreating back.

He stiffened yet didn't turn back.

"Can I help you?" the kid at the concession stand asked.

"I'll take a popcorn."

"With or without butter?"

Bliss choked back a sob, unable to answer the simple question.

"With," a male voice answered for her. "She'll take a soda, too."

Drake moved forward, handing the kid a ten.

"How do you know I want butter?" she asked, thinking it was better to project anger than hurt.

"Don't really care if you do or don't. I just want to watch you eat it." There was a tone to his voice that made a shiver run down her back to the base of her spine.

The student behind the counter turned bright red as he shoved popcorn into the cup and poured her soda. Reaching out, she took them, trying to ignore the part of herself that, so far, only one other man had managed to stir to life.

"Jace is hanging out with his friends tonight. Want to grab a burger at the diner after the game?"

Bliss watched Shade through the open doorway as he climbed back up the steps of the bleachers. Anything would be better than spending the rest of the night moping about what she didn't have anymore. Drake was a handsome man, and he might be just the distraction she needed for a couple of hours.

"Sure, I'm not doing anything. I'll meet you there. I came with my roommate, so I'll have to drop her off first."

"See you there in twenty minutes, then."

"Okay."

Bliss was aware of him watching her as she returned to her seat next to Ginny. He stood in the doorway, not taking his eyes off her as she ate the popcorn he had bought her. Teasingly, she licked the butter off her bottom lip before sliding the tip of the straw into her mouth.

"What about mine?"

"I forgot," Bliss stated truthfully. "Here, you can have mine."

"Never mind. It would have ruined my dinner, anyway."

"What are you doing for dinner?" Bliss asked absently, her attention on Drake.

"Lily, Beth, Winter, and Willa invited me to dinner at King's after the game."

Bliss frowned. "I thought Lily was home with John because he's sick."

"He's better, I guess. Shade thought he was running a fever at lunch today, but Lily stayed home and kept an eye on him all afternoon. Willa texted me while you were getting the popcorn to say who all was going, and she mentioned Lily, so his fever must have gone away."

"Fevers generally last longer than an hour."

Ginny shrugged. "Babies his age run fevers all the time. He's probably just teething."

"Maybe so."

Bliss searched the crowd for Shade, finding him sitting on the top row next to Jo Turner. *What could those two have to talk about?*

Jo's face was lit up like the Fourth of July at what Shade was saying to her. Rider and Train were sitting in front of them, blocking them from view. She had almost missed them herself. If she hadn't been looking for Shade in particular, she would have never noticed them.

Her jealousy over Shade was probably making her read more into it than there really was, and she had already learned that lesson. This time, she would mind her own business, despite the niggling feeling that something was up between the two. She didn't appear to be depressed over her father's murder a couple of months ago. Bliss couldn't help the snide thought.

"You ready?" Ginny stood, waiting. The game had ended, and she hadn't even noticed.

"Yes. Do you want me to drop you off at King's or the house?"

"King's, if you don't mind. Willa said she would give me a ride back. I'll try not to wake you when I come home."

"Don't worry about it. I'm going out myself. I probably won't be in until morning." Bliss didn't plan on hiding her active sex life from Ginny. She was used to getting a lot of sex, and it had been a while. She was going to break her dry spell that night. The surprising part was Ginny didn't bat an eyelash at her.

"Who are you going out with?"

Knowing Ginny was still determined to try to become BFFs with her, Bliss almost didn't tell her, but honestly, she couldn't find a reason not to. It wasn't like she was going to come home afterward and have a chat-fest about it.

"Drake Hall."

A concerned look crossed Ginny's face. "Be careful, Bliss."

Bliss couldn't help laughing. "I can handle Drake."

"Don't be too sure. He has a reputation in town for leaving women when they get too serious about him."

"Then he's perfect for me. I have no intention of getting serious."

Ginny shook her head at her. "That's what all the women say."

"Well, I mean it." Bliss watched as Shade stood, blending into the crowd and leaving the auditorium. Jo's eyes followed after him. "Besides, I can't give what's already taken."

Bliss started past her yet paused when Ginny laid a hand on her arm.

"You have an itch any man could scratch without leaving marks. Drake's not that type of man. Of all the women I heard gossip about regarding him, none have walked away unscathed. He's always been the one to break it off. Some scratches go away after a few days, and you forget they ever existed, but others fester and spread until they consume you."

"Are you telling me I should be afraid of him?" Bliss couldn't believe Ginny was giving her advice about men. Didn't she realize what went on in the clubhouse? What did she know about men, anyway? She was barely nineteen.

Willa had told her Ginny had lived with a foster couple until she had turned eighteen. Willa had wanted to help Ginny find a home she could call her own. Bliss knew that was why she had asked her if she would be interested in being roommates with Ginny.

Bliss had thought they were mismatched but grudgingly had begun to feel a tendril of liking for Ginny.

"That's exactly what I'm telling you. A smart woman would steer clear of him."

"No one's ever accused me of being smart," Bliss said wryly.

Chapter Four

The diner was crowded from the basketball game, but Drake was already seated at a table when she arrived. He stood as she approached, and when she stopped next to him, she felt surrounded by his size and couldn't help appreciating the way he looked in jeans and a dark T-shirt. She was used to confident men, and Drake was also assertive, which Bliss always enjoyed. It was going to be fun to find out if his confidence was deserved or not.

Once she slid into the booth, he sat down next to her. Bliss had to give him kudos, shy men didn't appeal to her.

"Hungry?"

Drake wasn't the only one who wasn't shy.

"I'm always hungry," she replied suggestively.

His gaze dropped to her lips. "Let's feed you, then." He motioned for the waitress to take their order.

"What can I get for you?" the waitress asked.

"I'll take a cheeseburger and fries. No onion."

"I'll take the same." Drake's amber-colored eyes stared intently into hers.

She was used to taking a backseat to what men wanted, like how she loved onions but never allowed herself to eat them because the men at the clubhouse would complain about the odor on her breath.

It was cute that he hadn't ordered onions on his burger. He was becoming more interesting than she had expected.

When the waitress left, Drake turned to face her in the booth, sliding his arm along the back until the pad of his thumb brushed her nape.

"I am going to be upfront with you before anything happens between us."

Here it comes, the 'I'm not going to get serious so don't expect a ring' speech.

"Let me save you the trouble," Bliss interrupted before he could begin. "I'm clean. I might have belonged to The Last Riders for a while, but I've always practiced safe sex." Well, she had once she had been rescued by The Last Riders. Then she had been tested because Stark never cared to use protection with her. "I expect you to use a condom each and every time. If you don't have any or run out, let me know, because I carry them in my purse. If we both run out, then you're shit out of luck. I don't fuck without a glove.

"Believe it or not, I'm not looking for a serious relationship, so we won't be doing sleepovers. If you're in the mood to fuck, send me a text. If I'm in the mood, I'll show. If not, I'm sure you have someone else who can.

"Anything pretty much goes with me concerning sex. I don't do bestiality, but if you've got another chick who turns me on and she's willing, I might give her a whirl, too. Let me think a second to make sure I've covered all the bases...Oh, yeah. If you ever lay a hand on me when you're mad, playtime is over."

Bliss forced herself to look up from the tabletop after she gave her speech, only to see the waitress gaping at her. It took a couple of seconds before she set the plates down in front of them then hurriedly escaped.

"Well, if I wasn't classified as a slut in this town before, I am now."

Drake's mouth twitched. "As she's one of the women I do occasionally, I'm sure she was stunned by your gracious offer to have a threesome."

Bliss picked up her burger and took a bite. "Not with her. She's not my type."

"Really. What type of women are you attracted to?"

"Preferably one who doesn't look at me like I'm Freddy Krueger."

Drake burst out laughing. "Finish your burger. Don't worry, I won't be asking Deb to join us. When I fuck, I like to devote my attention to one woman. I'm not sixteen anymore, I'm more interested in quality instead of quantity."

"Physical activity decreases the effects of aging."

"I'll keep that in mind when I drag my lazy ass out of bed to go to the gym in the mornings." As Drake took a bite of his own burger, his gleaming teeth had Bliss wishing he would bite down on something of hers.

They were almost finished with their meal when she looked up to see The Last Riders entering. She managed to swallow her bite of food and keep her gaze away from Jewell, Raci, Rider, Crash, and Train as they goofed around at a table not far from them.

Whereas Raci waved at her enthusiastically, Jewell was too busy studying Drake with appreciation to pay any attention to her. The men ignored her.

Bliss pushed her plate away.

"Finished?"

"Yes." She had suddenly lost her appetite.

"Good. Let's go." Drake picked up the check as he slid out of the booth. He took her arm and led her to the register. The weird thing was it didn't feel as if Drake was escaping the presence of the bikers, which was something she had come to expect from most of the townspeople.

He kept her close as he unhurriedly paid, casually waving at their waitress as he left while keeping one hand firmly on her arm as they went outside the door.

"Where are you parked?"

"Over there." Bliss nodded to her new blue Camry.

"Figured you for something flashier."

"What, a Porsche?"

"No, a Harley."

Bliss smiled. "I'm better at hanging on than driving a motorcycle myself."

They came to a stop beside her car and Drake placed a hand on the roof, pinning her against the door.

"Am I following you to your house?" she asked.

"No, I'm going to follow you to make sure you make it home safe."

"I thought we would—"

"Fuck?" Drake finished for her. "No. Like I tried to tell you inside the diner before you put words in my mouth, I don't fuck on the first date. How would I know what you like in bed if I don't know anything about you?" He molded his palm around the curve of her breast. "I'm tempted to forget that rule for you, but I won't." His thumb delved under her top to brush against her sensitive areola. "Women are to be savored like a fine wine, not guzzled like beer."

Bliss felt her knees weaken as her pussy clenched in need. His teasing touch had her hands going to his belt. She was sure she could tempt him enough to forget about that stupid rule.

Drake took a step forward, pinning her hands between their bodies. His hard cock nestled against her had her pussy weeping in misery. She tried to grind herself against him, but he caught her hips in a tight grip.

His amber gaze held her speechless as he lowered his head, the tip of his tongue licking the tender flesh under her earlobe. Her head fell back against the car.

"I don't fuck without a glove, either. If we decide to take this further, both of us will get tested."

Bliss opened her mouth to remind him she didn't want a relationship, but he cut her off.

"About you not wanting to be serious, I can't make any promises. I've wanted your pretty face on my pillow for a while, and I plan to be pretty serious when I'm pounding you into my mattress. If you can manage to crawl out of my bed to go home when I'm done with you, go for it."

He bit down on her earlobe, the flash of pain nearly making her come. "I'll take you up on the texting part. I'm not a dumbass. Except, when I text you that I want you, your ass better be there unless you have a good excuse, like being at work or having an accident and being in ICU."

Bliss liked a domineering man, and Drake was lighting her pussy up like a firecracker. If he turned out to be a dud in bed, she was afraid she would die of disappointment.

"I've already told you I don't do threesomes…the two- or four-legged kind. Let me think a minute on the other bullshit you were spouting off. Oh, yeah, I don't hit. If I want to punish you, I have a more effective way than one that will put my ass in jail." He rubbed his thumb over her nipple for a brief second again before removing his hand and straightening her top back in place. He took a step back from her, placing a small space between them. "Give me your cell phone."

Bliss reached into her jacket, taking out her cell and handing it to him. Within seconds, he had keyed in his number. Then she heard his phone ring from his pocket. He handed hers back after disconnecting the call.

"You doing anything tomorrow night?"

Bliss barely managed to squeak out a no.

"Want to go out?"

She nodded.

"Good. I'll pick you up around seven. We'll go dancing at the Pink Slipper." He reached around her, opening her car door. He then placed a chaste kiss against the corner of her mouth before going to his own car.

Bliss stood still, unable to calm her rioting body. She wasn't used to her body's needs not being taken care of. She didn't know if she could take it twice.

"Can I ask you a question?" she called out to him.

"Go ahead," he answered, turning back toward her.

"Do you fuck on the second date?"

Chapter Five

"What are your plans for tonight?" Bliss blew on her hot coffee as she waited for Ginny's answer.

"The same as last night, dinner and television. Why?"

"I invited Drake over for dinner." Bliss knew it was rude as hell to have asked Drake before talking it over with Ginny, but she was a woman in need, dammit.

She had expected him to fuck her the night they went out dancing, but he had left her at her door with another chaste kiss, which was beginning to irritate the shit out of her. It had only been a week and a half since they had started seeing each other, and to most women, that would seem too soon to fuck a man. To her, it was a week and a half too long.

"So, you want me to disappear for a few hours?"

"Preferably the whole night. It wouldn't bother me if you're in the house, but I thought it might bother you." Bliss took a sip of her coffee, trying not to feel guilty for putting her roommate on the spot.

Wait, since when did she care about another woman's feelings? Only one woman had managed to touch a spot in her heart, and that was Lily.

The night Lily had been in the fire at the clubhouse, she had unconsciously revealed her past to everyone living there. Her nightmarish childhood had roused Bliss's sympathy. It had helped her hold back her jealousy toward her until Lily had been threatening to leave Shade because of his past. Bliss remembered thinking, *Doesn't the woman understand loyalty?*

Bliss took another sip of her hot coffee, punishing herself with the burn because it turned out Lily *had* understood loyalty. She had been trying to protect Shade. By then, though, Bliss had made a fool of herself in front of him and the other club members, calling Lily a bitch and telling her she would be in a psych ward if it weren't for her husband.

"I appreciate the courtesy. I have a friend who will let me crash on her couch for the night." Ginny didn't seem too angry. In fact, the woman didn't have a temper at all as far as Bliss could tell.

Bliss had lived her life with numerous women, and Ginny was different from them all. If the woman hadn't told her that she didn't have sisters, Bliss would have thought she had lived with several. She was easygoing, never a picky bitch, wasn't nosy, and didn't mind if Bliss helped herself to her spare T-shirts when she was running behind on laundry. She was the perfect roommate for her.

"Thanks."

Bliss began planning what she would cook for dinner. It had to be something easy; she was a lousy cook and didn't want the night ruined by something burned.

She decided she would call King's restaurant later that afternoon and order two steaks and salads. She would also buy dessert at Willa's bakery.

"No problem. I don't mind this once." Ginny was letting her know she wasn't going to make a habit of leaving her home every time Bliss wanted to get laid.

Bliss smiled. "I think I'm beginning to like you."

Ginny smiled back. "Let me know when you make up your mind. I'll put you on my Christmas list."

"I love presents! Green is my favorite color. Red is my least."

"Okay...I'll tell Santa if he asks."

Bliss turned away, setting down her coffee cup. "He won't. I've been on Santa's naughty list so long they've taken my name off. Now, I need to get busy if I'm going to be ready for Drake to come."

"It's only eight in the morning."

"I know, but I have a lot to do."

Bliss escaped upstairs, where she straightened her room then vacuumed the whole floor. Ginny was always neat; Bliss was the messy one. When she dressed in the morning, even if she wasn't going out, she would try numerous outfits on until she was satisfied, leaving clothes strewn around the room. She hadn't vacuumed her room in a month, and the dust balls were peeking out from under the bed. She had been enjoying not having to clean.

When she lived at the clubhouse, it seemed like she was pulling that punishment or chore every week. It was strange, but she didn't mind the housework so much that morning.

Heading downstairs to start a load of laundry, she saw Ginny had cleaned the kitchen before going to work. The dirty coffee cups had disappeared, and the counters had been wiped down. So had the kitchen table that had become a catch-all for their mail and coupons, which Ginny painstakingly clipped every week, despite Bliss offering grocery money for food she didn't eat. Ginny had refused, saying throwing coupons away was like throwing money away. Bliss hadn't disagreed when she had handed over two coupons for her mac and cheese.

Starting the laundry, she went to the fridge to get a bottled water, finding a note on the refrigerator door Ginny had placed there.

All girls are on the good list.

Tell Santa that, Bliss thought to herself.

After the house was cleaned and the laundry done, she glanced at the time. Realizing it was already after four, she called in her food order then went back upstairs to get herself ready. She picked out a leather skirt and vest, thinking, *Drake won't be turning me down again*. They had been out on four dates, and if he didn't fuck her that night, she was done.

The man made her so horny she was tempted to take care of the problem herself. The only reason she hadn't, although she hated to admit it, was because of the anticipation.

If he told her one more time that he wanted to get to know her better, she was going to shock the shit out of him by ripping her clothes off. When she was done with him, he would know her in every possible way, including a few positions he had probably never thought of.

Staring at herself in the mirror, she adjusted her skirt until it was a little higher. Once she ran her hand through her gelled hair to spike it up farther, she was ready.

The doorbell rang as she was going down the steps.

Opening the door, she was greeted by Evie holding two large takeout bags. "Dinner to go."

Bliss took the bags from her before closing the door behind Evie, who had invited herself in.

"This looks like more than two steaks and salads," she said, carrying the bags into the kitchen with Evie following.

"I put in a couple of baked potatoes and some grilled corn. We had an extra raspberry cheesecake I brought, too."

"Let me get my wallet. You saved me a trip to Willa's bakery."

Bliss wasn't surprised Evie had shown up to find out the gossip about her and Drake. She had seen the curiosity in her eyes when Evie had seen them together at the diner for lunch earlier in the week.

None of the women had been forbidden to talk to her; however, they preferred hanging out with the men. She had been the same way when she had been a member. Evie, though, had been over to hang out a few times since The Last Riders had tossed her out.

Evie waved her hand. "Don't worry about it. It's on the house."

Abandoning her purse, Bliss opened all the containers and placed the food on serving dishes before putting them in the oven to keep warm.

"Drake doesn't know you can't cook?"

"I can cook," Bliss said self-consciously.

"Microwavable cups of macaroni and cheese and soup don't count."

"They count when you're hungry."

Evie shook her head, laughing. Then her expression turned serious. "You must like him if you don't want him to know you can't cook."

"He's sexy as hell, and I want to fuck him, but that's about the extent of my feelings for him." Bliss threw the restaurant bags away and began setting the table.

Evie watched as Bliss took a candle from the counter, placing it in the middle of the table.

"How is he in bed?"

Bliss avoided her gaze, biting her lip. "I don't know. I haven't fucked him yet."

Evie's mouth dropped open. "You've been out with him a couple of times, haven't you?"

"Four times, to be exact. This will make the fifth."

"So, what's the holdup?"

"He wants to get to know me better." Even to her own ears, it sounded as lame as when he had said it to her.

"There's no better way to get to know someone than fucking them."

"I told him that," Bliss agreed.

"Well, what did he say?"

"Nothing. He just smiled."

"That's strange."

"I thought so, too." Bliss nodded. "I've never dealt with a guy who put off fucking me. It's weird."

"You don't suppose...Never mind."

"What?" Bliss went to the refrigerator and took out a bottle of wine she had been chilling. Opening the bottle, she poured herself and Evie a glass. If they were going to dissect her semi-relationship with Drake, she wanted alcohol.

"I'm sure he's not, but..."

"What?" Bliss asked again.

"Do you think he's into dudes?"

"You *have* met Drake, haven't you?" There was no way Drake was into dudes. The man screamed sex on a stick, and she wanted to lick him like a popsicle.

"I've seen him a time or two at the restaurant."

"He's not gay," Bliss said emphatically, her mind going back over her last date with Drake.

They had gone to one of the high school fundraisers. Drake was on the school board and had felt it his duty to participate. It was a pizza dinner, and she had helped him make over sixty pizzas, leaving them covered in sweat and marinara by the time they were done. She was disappointed when he drove her home instead of taking her back to his place.

"Winter thought Viper was gay when he was fucking all the women at the clubhouse," Bliss thought out loud. "Drake was seeing a waitress at the diner before we started going out. Maybe he's giving it to her instead of me."

"Or the busboy."

"Will you shut up? He's not into dudes."

"Bliss, if he hasn't tried to fuck you yet, he's into dudes."

ꕥ

"This is really good," Drake complimented.

"I'm glad you like it. Would you like some more?"

"No, thanks. I've had enough." Drake placed his fork on his plate before rising to collect his dirty dishes.

"I was going to do that."

He ignored her protest, placing his dishes in the sink. "I don't need you to wait on me." He then began washing them.

After Bliss carried her dishes to him, he loaded the dishwasher and started it.

"Want to watch a movie?"

"I want to fuck." The stubborn look on her face tested his willpower. He had to admit it was becoming difficult to resist a woman so determined to have his body.

His expression became closed as he leaned back against the counter, crossing his arms against his chest. "You're a feisty little thing, aren't you?"

Bliss stiffened. "Don't patronize me. I don't like it."

His expression became cold. "I'm not patronizing you. When I do, believe me, you will know it."

There was a difference between being cute and being a bitch. He had married one, resulting in being divorced before he was twenty. As cute as Bliss was when she was bitchy, it didn't tempt him to unsnap his jeans.

Bliss barely seemed to be holding on to her temper. "What's your problem?"

"Sit." He didn't raise his voice, yet he noticed the hint of command made her knees tremble.

He knew her body was fighting the instinct to obey him, but she was unable to keep herself from going to the table and sitting down.

"You're very sexually oriented, aren't you?"

Bliss frowned across the room at him. "What does that mean?"

"That you're used to having sex regularly."

"Then, yes."

"How much?"

"That's kind of personal..." Bliss evaded.

"You don't strike me as being shy."

"I'm not," she admitted. "When I lived at the clubhouse, I was used to having sex any time I wanted it. Does that answer your question?"

Yes, it did, and he wasn't surprised. He had heard the gossip around town without taking part in it. He really didn't care how many men she had fucked before him as long as she didn't continue to since he was seeing her. That was a deal breaker for him.

"How often since you left the clubhouse?"

"None."

That was what he had hoped to hear.

"Is that why you want to have sex with me, because you're horny?"

"Yes."

"I see." Drake stared at the little blonde glaring back at him petulantly. He wanted to fuck her senseless, but that wouldn't accomplish his goal. If he stood there much longer, though, his resolve was going to break.

She had lost her bitchy attitude and was back to being cute.

Drake gripped each side of the counter, his knuckles white from the pressure he exerted. "It's time I left. I need to pick Jace and Cal up from work. Their car wouldn't start, so I'm playing chauffeur until Jo's finished with the repairs."

Bliss jumped up from the chair. "I thought Stephanie was picking them up and dropping them off at your house."

"I'm going to save her the trip." Drake carefully released the counter after he regained enough self-control, brushing past her as he headed for the living room.

"Wait!" Bliss grabbed his arm. "I don't understand. Why are you leaving? Aren't you attracted to me?" Her confused expression had his dick pressing against the zipper of his jeans.

"Bliss, this isn't the time—"

Her hand dropped from his arm. "You don't have to say anything else. I understand."

Drake stopped. "You do?"

"Yes, you should have told me. I'm cool with it."

"With what?"

"You're gay. I can see how it would be difficult to come out in a small town like Treepoint."

"I'm not gay. You think I'm gay?" He wasn't insulted, but he thought it was sad as hell that the only reason she could think of for why he wasn't having sex with her was because she believed he was gay.

"Not many men run away when I ask them to fuck me."

"I'm not running away." Drake shoved his hands in his pockets to keep himself from spanking her ass. "I'm just not going to become a dildo to get you off because The Last Riders got tired of you."

She jerked as if he had struck her. "I think you're right, it's time you left." She moved past him to open the door.

"Bliss..." His anger at her dissipated. He had seen the puppy-dog eyes that had followed after Shade the night of the basketball game, so he should have realized the remark would cut her deeply. Drake intended to be in her bed; he just wasn't going to be at her beck and call simply because she no longer had the one she wanted there.

"Good night."

Drake sighed. The only way to calm her down at that point would be to give in and take her to bed, and if he did that, then everything he had been trying to accomplish with the little spitfire would be lost.

"Good night, Bliss. I'll give you a call tomorrow."

"You do that," Bliss snapped before slamming the door in his face.

Drake almost opened the door and showed the woman she had nearly pushed him too far. As an alternative, he went to his car, sliding behind the wheel.

Bliss had no idea she was pushing him. When she did, she would realize how kind he had been. Regardless, if she kept it up, she would find out he had a way of dealing with her that would put her where she belonged—in his bed, begging him for forgiveness.

He drove through town, first picking up Jace at Pizza Shop, where he was making pizzas instead of delivering them due to the car issue, and then swinging by to pick up Cal from the grocery store. The boys filled him in on their days as he travelled the dark streets toward his home.

Making a left, he drove up the side road that led him through the affluent area of town. The houses grew larger and farther apart as he continued down the street. Drake made a left onto the last driveway, seeing a red sports car sitting there.

His lips tightened when he saw his ex-wife sitting behind the wheel.

Drake parked his car next to hers.

"Why is she here?" Jace groaned. "I called and told her you were picking us up. I have homework. I can't deal with her tonight."

"Go inside. She's not here to see you."

The boys climbed out of the car. Jace flung his hand up in a wave toward his mother as his only acknowledgment of her before going into the house with Cal. Drake knew he wasn't going to be as lucky.

Getting out of the car, he made sure to press the lock button. Stephanie had gone through his car several times when she wanted to snoop into his life. He then walked toward his front door without giving her a glance.

"Drake! We need to talk." Stephanie jumped out of her car.

"We have nothing to talk about. Jace has homework."

"Drake, please, can't I at least come in? We need to talk."

Despite knowing the manipulative bitch she was, how she could look all soft and sweet still surprised him.

"We have nothing to say. The last time I let you in to talk about Jace, it took me a week to get you out." The manipulative bitch had pretended to trip over an extension cord and sprain her ankle. She had spent the week in his spare bedroom, until he had thrown her ass out.

"I'm not here to talk about Jace. I want to talk about the new woman you've been seeing."

"It's none of your business."

Stephanie ran a shaky hand through her dyed platinum-blonde hair. "I heard you're seeing that slut from The Last Riders. Is it true?"

"Her name is Bliss, and you're the last person who should be calling another woman a slut."

"I don't want her around my son."

"Why?" With each woman he dated, she had a different reason for him to stop seeing them. It was usually worse when she was between men. And Jace had told him after his last visit to her house that her husband of two years had moved out, which meant she was between men at that moment.

"Because she's a slut, and Jace is at an impressionable age. I don't plan on my son getting his sexual education from a woman like that."

"You're really fucked-up, you know that?" He would rather have Bliss tell him honestly about her sexual past than a woman like Stephanie, who would still attempt to pretend she was a virgin if everyone in town didn't know Jace was her son and she had been married numerous times.

"Don't talk like that to me! I have the right to control who is or isn't allowed around my son!"

"You didn't give a damn about bringing in every asshole in Treepoint and fucking them behind my back when he was a kid."

"I told you it was only one time."

"Stephanie, you don't have to lie anymore. We're not married. I quit caring how many men had fucked you when I walked in and saw Jared fucking you doggy-style while my kid was eating a bowl of cereal in the kitchen!"

Stephanie had probably been with as many men as Bliss, but she considered herself above her. She was lying even to herself. Bliss, on the other hand, was blunt about what she wanted from him, making no effort to lie about the men in her past. She painted the darkest picture of herself and made no apologies about it. He could still see her defiant face when she had told him about having sex with all of The Last Riders. Truth he could respect; it was lies that destroyed.

His ex-wife took a step forward, pressing her breasts against him. "Please, Drake, I've never gotten over you. I made a terrible mistake—"

"Yes, you did. You made another if you think I would ever give you another chance. I've told you to keep your nose out of my business. Bliss is no concern of yours. Don't make me regret giving you visitation with Jace."

"He's almost eighteen. It will be up to him how often he sees me."

"Yes, it will," Drake agreed, knowing Stephanie would be lucky to see Jace once a year when the decision was left up to him.

"I didn't come by to start an argument. If you change your mind, just call me. I'm willing to take you any way I can get you, Drake."

"I won't be calling. I'm giving you a heads-up now. I like Bliss, and I plan on seeing more of her. I don't want you to give her any shit. If you do, you'll be dealing with me, and you know how I'll deal with you, don't you?"

Since Jace lived with him full–time, he didn't have to pay child support. In fact, she owed him a large amount he had never collected on in order to stop her from the continued threats of taking him back to court for more visitations and to lower her child support payments. She owed him a huge sum of money, and with Jace being so close to eighteen, her threats of getting more visitations were going to be ignored. If she messed with Bliss, however, he would go after her for the money.

He was looking forward to when Jace turned eighteen. Then he would let the boy handle his mother himself and cut his last connection with her.

Stephanie went pale at the threat, taking a step back. "For Christ's sake, she lived with a biker gang. That trash doesn't need you to defend her. She won't make you happy. No one woman is capable of making you happy. I should know, I tried hard enough."

"You want to make me happy, Stephanie? Stay away from me."

"I still love you."

Drake shook his head. "You don't love me. You became pregnant after swearing you were on the pill. I was stupid enough to believe you and put a ring on your finger. You told me lie after lie, and I always believed you. The men, the money you were always promising Jace when he needed something…You couldn't tell the truth if your life depended on it." He had sworn to himself to never tolerate another woman lying to him ever again. "You're still lying. The only difference is I'm not a kid anymore, and I don't give a fuck." Drake turned, not caring if she had anything else to say. He had already given her more of his time than she deserved.

She had done him one favor—his dick was no longer driving him crazy. Any desire for caving in and returning to Bliss's house had died when Stephanie opened her mouth.

Drake shook his head at himself as he walked inside and slammed the door on Stephanie's lying face. He had obviously made a habit of picking complicated women. He needed to warn Jace. If he had inherited Drake's propensity for choosing aggravating women, he was heading for trouble.

"God help him, because he's going to need all the help he can get."

Chapter Six

"Going out?"

Bliss watched in the mirror as Ginny threw herself on the bed, settling herself comfortably.

"Yes, I'm going to Rosie's. Want to go?"

"I'll pass. I don't like going to bars."

"Why not?"

"They're pick-up joints."

"Yes, they are." Bliss smoothed her red top down to show more of her cleavage. Her black leather pants and knee-high boots perfectly accentuated her diminutive figure.

"Aren't you seeing Drake?"

"Not anymore. I'm tired of waiting for him to put out."

"You're breaking up with him because he won't have sex with you?"

"Pretty much," Bliss confirmed.

"Why?"

"I just told you."

Ginny sat up on the side of the bed. "No woman breaks up with a man for not having sex."

"I do." Bliss turned away from the mirror and picked up her purse, ignoring Ginny's narrow-eyed stare. "I won't be back tonight. I'll see you tomorrow or whenever."

"Bliss, you can't just go home with someone you don't know. It's not safe."

"Don't worry, I use protection."

"That's good, but that's not what I'm talking about, and you know it." Ginny shook her head. "You always do that, Bliss. You become a smart-ass when you know it's something you shouldn't be doing."

"Why shouldn't I go to a bar and pick up a guy? Men do it all the time. Why is it any different for a woman?"

Ginny's face held such sadness that even Bliss's cold heart was touched. "Because women leave a piece of themselves behind with each man, whether it's taken or given. Women aren't hardwired for emotionless sex."

"I am," Bliss denied Ginny's assertion.

"I don't believe that. I believe that's what you tell yourself to keep your heart from breaking."

"Geez, don't try to make a mountain out of a molehill. I'm going to get laid. When it's over, I'll come home and won't be any different than before I left."

Ginny stood up, going to her bedroom door. "Keep telling yourself that and you may make yourself believe it, but I won't. You're a nice person, despite how hard you try to hide it."

"No, I'm not. Every woman at the clubhouse who tried to be my friend will tell you that."

Sadly, Ginny shook her head. "All the wives, I'm sure, but what about the women who weren't old ladies? What would they say about you?" She didn't give Bliss time to answer, closing the door behind her.

Bliss pressed her fingers against the bridge of her nose as she fought back the twinge of pain she was beginning to feel in the region of her heart. She wasn't going to cry. She hadn't cried for herself in years, and she wasn't going to start then…well, except for the day she had gotten kicked out of The Last Riders.

Going downstairs, she went through the front door without a backward glance at Ginny's recriminating face. She had nothing to feel guilty about.

The drive to Rosie's was a short ten minutes, and the parking lot was filled with familiar motorcycles.

Bliss parked her car to the side before striding confidently into the busy bar. The Last Riders took up the first half of the establishment, sitting at the tables and at the bar. She walked past them as if they didn't exist, going to the other side of the room to take a seat at the bar.

"What can I get you, Bliss?" Mick, the bar owner, greeted her with a friendly smile.

"I'll take a beer."

She ran an experienced eye over the men sitting nearby. There wasn't much to choose from. In fact, the pickings were pretty slim. She hated fucking weak men, which they all were; she liked it when the men were strong enough to pick her up. She didn't want coyote ugly, either.

"Here you go." Mick placed her beer in front of her, and Bliss went to dig some cash out of her purse. "No charge."

Bliss gave Mick a sweet smile. "Thanks, Mick."

"No problem. You're good for business." He winked before moving along to wait on another customer.

"I was going to offer to buy you a beer, but Mick already took care of it." The male voice caught her attention, and she turned to see Greer Porter take a stool next to hers.

Bliss lifted the bottle to her lips, taking a long drink. "You can buy me my second one."

"That works for me." Greer grinned before taking a sip of his own beer.

"You here with your brothers?"

"Nope. Tate is holed up with his new girlfriend, and Dustin's working, trying to save up some money for Christmas presents." The expression on his face made her laugh.

"You don't like Christmas?"

"Don't like spending hard-earned money for presents that aren't going to be remembered the next day."

"Depends on the present," Bliss said suggestively.

Greer looked her over from head to toe, the sexual interest in his eyes increasing. "Yes, it does. I know I'd never forget anything you gave me."

Bliss lifted her beer toward him. "Let's make it a night neither one of us will ever forget."

ꕥ

Drake was watching television when he heard the knock at his front door. Standing up, he hoped it was Bliss, who hadn't answered his calls all day. He was going to give her another day to get over her anger before going by her house. He was glad she had stopped by to see him first.

When he opened the door to see his cousin Rachel, he tried to hide his disappointment. However, his perceptive cousin wasn't easily fooled.

"What's wrong?"

"Nothing. I just thought you were someone else." He should have known the little firecracker wasn't going to get over him throwing The Last Riders at her. She might no longer be one of them, but her loyalty remained with the club.

"I'm sorry." Despite her words, Rachel's happiness shined through her beautiful eyes.

"Forget about it and come in. Tell me what has you so damn happy."

Rachel walked inside, tugging off her thick coat. "Don't be so grumpy. It's not my fault Bliss isn't here."

Drake narrowed his eyes at her. "What makes you so sure it was Bliss I was hoping to see?"

"Well, wasn't it?"

"Yes, but that doesn't mean you always have to be right," Drake snapped.

"You're in a terrible mood. I'll come back when you're in a better one." Rachel began to put her coat back on, but Drake took it away before gently gripping her arm and leading her to the couch.

"Sit down and tell me why you're at my house at nine o'clock at night."

Rachel sat down, grinning up at him. "All right, you forced me!" Rachel quipped. "Cash and I are expecting." She was practically bouncing on the couch cushions.

Drake bent down to lift her up, giving her a bear hug. "Congratulations, Rachel. I couldn't be happier for you and Cash."

His cousin had married the notorious ladies' man of Treepoint after Cash had nearly managed to lose her following his blowout when he told practically the whole town he had slept with her. The Porter brothers had been so angry at her that Rachel had run off. If Cash hadn't crashed his motorcycle, Drake didn't think Rachel would be sitting next to him right then, glowing with contentment.

"Thank you. Cash wants a boy, but I want a little girl to drive him crazy."

Drake agreed. Cash deserved a little payback for driving all the fathers in Treepoint crazy.

He released Rachel to take a seat next to her on the couch.

"How's everything going with you?" she asked.

"Everything's good. Business is great."

"How about your personal life? Anyone you're serious about?"

"What's for me to tell? Seems you already know I'm seeing Bliss."

"I'm just curious how serious you are about her."

"Since when have you ever been curious about who I'm seeing?"

A tinge of red flooded her cheeks.

"Come on, Rachel. Why did you stop by so late to tell me your good news? You could easily have told me this morning when you saw me at the diner."

"I forgot and thought I'd stop by tonight, instead."

"All right." Drake didn't believe her for a split second.

"So, how serious are you about Bliss?"

That time, Drake saw the hesitation she was trying to hide in her eyes.

"Tell me," he ordered.

Rachel sighed. "I never was any good at keeping a secret. I talked to Cash an hour ago. He's at Rosie's with the guys. Bliss is in there, snuggled up against Greer. If you're not serious about her, then never mind. If you *are* serious about her, I thought you should know."

"How long ago was this?" She had told him she hadn't been with anyone since she had left The Last Riders. Obviously, if she couldn't get him to end her dry spell, she was going to find someone else.

"Cash called again right before I knocked. She's still there. After Stephanie, I thought you deserved to know before—"

"Before I made a fool of myself again?"

"That wasn't what I was going to say," Rachel denied quickly.

"You didn't have to," Drake said grimly as he stood up. "I need to leave. Could you do me a big favor?" He waited for her nod. "Jace and Cal are upstairs playing video games. Could you take them to your house for the night?"

Rachel raised a brow. "They're old enough to be alone while you're gone—"

"They may be, but I'm not coming back alone," he promised, though more to himself than her.

Rachel caught his arm before he could leave. "Be careful, Drake. You know Greer has a mean temper. He's like a grouchy bear if you try to take something he wants."

"You've never been to my hunting lodge, have you?"

"No, why?"

"You and Cash should go sometime. I love to show off my trophies. My favorite is a bear I caught two years ago. Don't worry, I can handle Greer."

Drake left Rachel with her mouth hanging open.

Chapter Seven

"Thirsty?" Greer asked as he led Bliss from the dance floor back to the bar.

"I'm always thirsty," Bliss replied as she slid onto the bar stool seductively.

Greer's gaze didn't leave her cleavage as he leaned against the counter near her. "We can't have that." He motioned to Mick to bring another beer.

"I think you're just the man to quench my thirst." Bliss moved her hand to Greer's belt, tugging him closer to her side.

"Woman, you're playing with fire."

"I've never been afraid of being burned. Besides, my panties are flame resistant," she teased.

"They'd have to be with a hot piece like you."

Bliss's provocative smile slipped when the bar door opened and Drake strode inside. The expression on his face had her body stiffening.

What the fuck is he doing here? In all the years she had been coming to Rosie's, she had never seen him inside the bar.

He scanned the crowd as if looking for someone. Surely he wasn't looking for her, was he? How would he have even known she was there? What would it have mattered to him, anyway?

She leaned closer to Greer, hoping his body would block her from view.

"Woman, I like going fast, too, but I've never been one for going at it in public. But hell, I'm game if you are." Greer slid his hand up her arms before pressing her closer to his chest.

"Let her go, Greer. Now."

A voice so cold that ice ran through her blood came from behind her, and it had both her and Greer stiffening.

"Go away, Drake, and mind your own business." Greer didn't release her.

"It's my business when you're holding my woman."

Oh, shit! Bliss frantically tried to gather her frightened thoughts. Something about Drake's attitude was sending panic through her bloodstream. No man had ever called her *his woman*. The most Stark had done to claim her was call her his bitch.

"She ain't yours. She's been rubbing against me all night like a cat in heat. No woman who belongs to another man behaves like that."

"She does when she doesn't know who she belongs to. She'll learn that lesson tonight and never forget it again. You, on the other hand, need to let her go and get the hell out of here, or cousin or not, Tate will be coming to drive you to the ER."

Bliss felt Greer release her, his body shifting away from hers.

"You're not going to fight him over me?" Bliss asked in disbelief. Everyone in town knew the Porters used any excuse for a fight.

"Hell no. Drake's my cousin. Kin don't fight over women."

"Just a few minutes ago, you were promising to fuck me into tomorrow. What happened to that?" Bliss snapped at the good-looking man who was slipping farther away from her.

"Sorry about that, Drake. Didn't know she was yours."

Greer's apology had Bliss grinding her teeth in frustration.

"You two are kidding me, right? Drake doesn't want me, and the one who does won't do anything about it, because you're like a dog that has a bone and doesn't want it anymore but doesn't want anyone else to touch it." Bliss slid angrily off the stool. "Well, fuck you both. I'm going home."

Drake caught her arm. "You're right about that. Let's go."

Bliss found herself ushered toward the door. The Last Riders sitting at the table watched as her feet did double-time, trying to keep up.

"Rider, stop him." Her heels tried to dig into the floor as she futilely attempted to pull away.

A wave of his hand was his only response.

She started to yell for Shade, who was sitting at a table with Cash, but she knew it would be useless.

"Train, could you help—"

"Drake looks like he has it under control," Train called out.

Dammit, how could they just sit there and watch?

She tried to grab a beer bottle from a table close by. She would brain the fucker herself. Her fingertips only managed to knock the bottle over, and she found herself clutching air instead.

Before she could yell at Crash or Moon, Drake had pulled her through the door to the parking lot.

"What are you doing? Have you lost your mind?" Since when did the charming man she had been seeing become as forceful as a biker?

Drake came to a stop next to his sports car. Opening the door, he stared down at her grimly. "Get in."

"Kiss my ass."

He gently cupped her cheek. "Get in or go back inside. Not a man inside will touch you after I called you mine."

"The Last Riders aren't afraid of you," Bliss snapped.

"No, they're not, but I didn't see a man in there taking up for you, either."

"I'm going home," Bliss said stubbornly, smothering the hurt feelings that once, they would have taken up for her en masse.

"Then go. It's your choice to make. Which is it going to be?"

"Are we going to fuck?"

She could see the fury darken his eyes. Bliss had to admit it gave him a dangerous look that would have sent her panties simmering if she had been wearing any.

"Yes, Bliss, I'm going to fuck you."

Bliss almost grinned. Greer was good-looking, but Drake had something that appealed to her—namely a six-two, rockin'-hard body she wanted to climb to reach that mouth and suck that bottom lip like a piece of candy. His soft touches and chaste kisses had kept her body in a state of arousal, sending her pussy quivering without even trying, while he hadn't even sported a hard-on behind those jeans he looked damned good wearing.

"I'll go with you, then." She started to get in his car.

"You sure?"

His eyes were warning her, but she had played every game with The Last Riders and the Devil's Rejects. Drake didn't have anything up his sleeve she hadn't experienced before.

"I'm sure."

The car door slammed as she buckled her seat belt.

As she watched Drake walk around the front of his car, Bliss saw Shade walk out of Rosie's. Drake paused in front of the car, waiting for Shade's reaction. Both men looked at her, and Bliss waved her hand at Shade. He nodded, giving Drake a warning gaze before going back inside.

Drake climbed in behind the wheel, closing his own door. Bliss was still staring at the door where Shade had disappeared.

"Something still going on between you and Shade?"

"No." Her voice broke.

"Then what was that about?"

Bliss shrugged. "He was making sure I was where I wanted to be."

"And are you?"

Bliss leaned her head back against the headrest. "For now."

She shivered as she watched his experienced hands put the car in gear and back out of the parking spot. She loved riding on the back of a bike, but watching Drake drive was surprisingly erotic. He held the power of the car in check as they roared down the mountain roads.

"Cold?" Drake turned the heat up higher. That was the last thing she needed right then.

"No, I'm fine." She stared at his shadowed face curiously. "How did you know I was at the club?"

"Rachel stopped by the house, and she mentioned Cash had told her you were there."

"Oh." Bliss didn't know whether to be angry or thankful to Rachel for telling on her.

"Why did you go there?"

"I like Rosie's. I go there a lot."

"Not anymore, unless I'm with you."

She would do what she damn well wanted to, but she wasn't about to start an argument with him before she had fucked him. Right after he took care of the ache in her pussy, she would tell him so.

When he pulled into his driveway, she almost jumped out of the car, anxious as she reached for the door handle.

"Sit still."

Drake's tone had her wanting to scream in frustration at him. Instead, she meekly played along as he got out of the car and came around to open the door.

She took the hand he offered as she climbed out, and he didn't release it as they walked toward his front door.

Bliss wanted to snatch her hand away. She wasn't exactly the hand-holding type. That was another lesson she would have to give him. She was beginning to think she was putting up with a lot of crap just to get laid. *He had better be good.*

Drake opened his front door, saying, "Bliss?"

"Don't worry, I'll be quiet. I won't wake Jace and Cal."

"They aren't home. I sent them to spend the night with Rachel." He shook his head at her. "You always put words in my mouth. We're going to have to work on that. What I was going to ask was, are you sure you want to do this?"

"I'm sure." Bliss started to go inside, but his arm came out, stopping her.

"I'm not Shade."

She gave him an angry glare. "Believe me, I know you're no Shade."

His hand dropped so she could go inside. Drake followed behind her, closing and locking the door. For some strange reason, the sound sent a warning chill down her spine. Moreover, the look on his face was one she had never seen there before.

A split second later, she was pinned against the wall with Drake holding her up high enough that her feet were off the floor.

"Sweet Bliss, that was the last time I ever want to hear his name on your lips."

Chapter Eight

Drake saw the arousal in Bliss's eyes. She expected him to fuck her against the wall. She believed she had won. She didn't know him at all. Her relationships had all revolved around sex, and when he wouldn't give her that, it had left her adrift. He was going to give her what she wanted, because he had pushed her too far while trying to wait for her to get over Shade.

Any good hunter knew it was time to change his hunting method if what he was doing wasn't working. Bliss needed to believe she was in control. He could give her that...*for now*.

He didn't give her his mouth. Holding her against the wall with one hand, he used the other to lift her top, exposing her breasts. Tugging it upward, he sucked a nipple roughly into his mouth, laving the tip into a hard bead. Then he used his teeth to graze the sensitized nipple, and Bliss arched her hips against his dick.

Drake lifted his head, letting her feet drop back to the floor. Roughly, he unbuttoned her tight leather pants and pulled them down her hips.

"How in the hell did you get into these?" he asked as he went to his haunches to peel them down.

"It wasn't easy." She stepped out of one leg then the other with his help.

"Bliss, nothing about you is easy." Drake slung the pants away, still eye-level with her shaved pussy. "I have to admit that was worth the effort, though." He leaned forward, letting his tongue slide along her slit. She was wet and tasted like pure bliss.

"I don't have to ask how you got your nickname, I can taste it, it's more addicting than Tate's finest."

"I'll take that as a compliment, I think." Bliss gasped.

"Believe me." Drake's tongue twirled against the engorged bud. "Nothing equals your pussy."

Drake played with her clit until he heard small gasps coming from between from her lips. It was a start, but not enough. He wanted her screaming.

Using his fingers to part the fleshy lips, he blew on her clit until he saw the little pearl glistening with need. He rubbed his finger against it, wetting it enough to insert into her. Instead of plunging deep, he explored the walls of her sheath, tantalizing nerve endings already quivering to come.

Expertly finding the spot he was searching for, he rubbed his knuckle against her G-spot. The screams he was waiting for erupted from her throat as she clenched around his finger in a tight hold with strong muscles that didn't want to let him go.

Bliss almost ripped his hair out as she tried to tug him upward. "I need you inside of me." Her demand was hoarse as her blue-colored eyes stared pleadingly, her hands becoming even more frantic.

When Drake stood, unzipping his jeans and pulling out his cock, her eyes widened and her mouth dropped. Drake smiled wryly. That wasn't the first time he had seen that look on a woman's face.

"I've died and gone to heaven," she proclaimed.

Drake took a condom out of his back pocket, tearing it open before he rolled it onto his large cock. Then, pressing his chest against hers, he lifted a slim thigh to his hip. His cock nudged her pussy and Bliss wiggled, trying to fit the tip into her opening.

"It won't fit," she whined.

"It'll fit." Drake pressed harder against her, using his body to hold her in place as he lifted her other thigh over his arm, spreading her wider.

Thrusting forward, he managed to push the bulb of his cock inside of her, causing another scream to fill the air as she clutched his shoulders.

"Oh, God. Oh, God," Bliss moaned, trying to adjust herself, but she couldn't move. Drake handled her easily, though, and her head rolled back and forth on the wall.

"Take it easy. Let me do all the work."

"That's easy for you to say! It's not going to fit!" Bliss panted, trying to use her hands on his shoulders to gain leverage.

Drake brushed his mouth against her collarbone, tracing up to her neck then the lobe of her ear. "You're going to take me. Then I'm going to carry you to my bed and fuck you again."

"I didn't even know cocks could be that big."

"It runs in the family." Drake laughed as he pumped his dick slowly higher inside of her.

Tiny beads of sweat broke out on her temple, dampening her hair.

"Oh, God, it's not normal. How do you even walk?"

"You're the one who's going to have trouble walking tomorrow." Drake brought his hand down between them, swirling his finger in the wetness he found there, and then he used it to wet the stalk of his cock. He slid inside another inch.

Bliss's tits shook at her accelerated breathing, tempting him.

"I have some pretty nipple clamps I'm going to put on these little cherries."

She became excited by his comment, enabling him to give her more of himself as he began pumping steadily. He wasn't gentle with her, inexorably pushing more and more of his slick dick inside of her.

Biting down on the side of her neck, he gave her a warning. "I'm going to give you the rest of it, and you're going to take it. You're sucking my dick in like you can't get enough."

"Believe me, I've had more than enough! Wait a second. Let me catch my breath."

"Then you better hurry and take a deep breath." Drake plunged deep inside her with a strong thrust, burying himself to the hilt in her tight pussy.

He groaned, trying to hold back his climax.

Giving her a minute, he rested against her. "All right?"

Her head lay limply against his shoulder.

He turned his head to look down at her. "Bliss?"

"I didn't believe it was possible."

"What?"

"To be fucked to death."

Drake laughed. "I think you'll survive." He began to fuck her slowly, using his hips to direct his cock to hit different spots in her pussy, building the fire he felt inside her.

"Faster."

"You beginning to like it?"

"Are you crazy? I liked it from the moment you pulled it out of your pants. I just didn't want to be torn in two trying to take it. No orgasm is worth dying for," she quipped.

"It's not over yet."

"Oh, God."

Drake stroked faster, building her climax to a height that had them clinging slickly together. He felt the walls of her pussy clenching him as he thrust deeper. Her screams were falling from her lips at a higher frequency.

He let one of her thighs go so she could grip him for leverage. Her arms circled his neck, and she began fucking him back.

Gripping her buttocks in his hands, he controlled her movements. "You'll hurt yourself."

"I don't care," she panted.

"I thought you said no orgasm was worth dying over," Drake reminded her.

"If it's my last one, I'm going to make it good."

Drake barely managed to hold on to the wild woman in his arms. If it went on much longer, she really would hurt herself.

He brought his hand to her clit, giving it the attention it needed to bring her to a shuddering peak. The feeling of her sharp little teeth biting into his shoulder had his cock stroking out a climax that wrenched a tortured groan from his own throat.

When Bliss's trembling slowed, he placed her on her feet then slowly let his dick slip from her before taking a step back. Bliss collapsed to the floor.

Drake removed the condom, going into the half bath to dispose of it before returning to see her still sitting on the floor in a daze.

"I just gave you what any man could give you." His sharp gaze didn't miss the wince his words had caused.

Bending down, he picked her up and carried her to his bedroom as she rested sweetly in his arms. Laying her gently down on the bed, he went into his bathroom and wet a washcloth with warm water before coming back to sit on the side of the bed. Then he softly ran the damp cloth over her bright pink pussy, cleaning her and letting the warmth ease the ache she was sure to be feeling.

"Better?"

"Yes, thank you."

Drake went back into the bathroom to toss the washcloth into the hamper, giving her a brief respite. He then took off his clothes and stepped into the shower, washing off while regretting the soap was also taking away the smell of Bliss.

She was everything he had anticipated when he had watched her trailing along with The Last Riders. Always mixed in with the other women in the club, she had drawn his attention with the air of loneliness that surrounded her.

At one of the football games, he was watching her when a little boy had become lost. Drake was already headed toward the wailing child. No one else had noticed in her group, who were watching the game. Bliss noticed, though, and went to the little boy, crouching down to talk to him.

Drake stopped to watch her. She had gone from seductive vixen in her tight leather pants to taking the terrified child's hand with a gentle smile and leading him to a security guard standing nearby. Bliss then remained with the child while the parents were located.

The mother, instead of being grateful, gave a look of horror that Bliss was touching her child. Bliss quietly left without receiving a thank-you as the security guard basked in the parents' gratitude.

The bikers were idiots to let her go. Their mistake was to his benefit, though—and Bliss's, if she would get her mind out of her panties long enough to realize just how good it could be between them. Her fiery spirit was twice as big as her small stature, and she was hell-bent on keeping their relationship casual, while the more time he spent with her, the more he wanted her.

Getting out of the shower, he dried off before hanging up his wet towel. Then he went back into the bedroom and saw her dozing on his bed. He almost hated to wake her up.

Sitting down next to her, he took off her top that was more off than on. Her eyes opened sleepily to gaze up at him.

"Hell no." Her grumpy voice brought a sensual smile to his lips.

"Oh, yes." His arousal was more than obvious and trepidation entered her eyes, which didn't lift from his cock.

Drake lay down next to her, gathering her into his arms. That time, he took her mouth in a kiss that had her head falling back onto the pillow. She circled her arms around his neck as her tongue entered his mouth. He slid his tongue along the side of hers, letting her take possession as she explored and discovered how he tasted.

Bliss's tiny nipples stood up, begging for attention. Breaking away from her mouth, he played with them using the tip of his tongue, suckling on each one until she moaned her pleasure and began lifting her hips.

"You ready for me again?"

"I can't believe I'm saying this, but…fuck me, Drake."

"You sure?"

"Dammit, just fuck me before I change my mind."

Drake licked his way from one nipple to the other. "I think I can guarantee that won't happen."

That time, when he went down on her, he used his teeth and tongue, rebuilding her desire until she was grasping the blanket in a death grip.

Reaching into his nightstand, he pulled out a condom, and a tube of lubricating cream. He rolled on the condom, then smeared a generous amount onto his condom-covered cock.

"You could have done that before!" Bliss accused.

Drake ignored her, sliding intimately between her thighs. Winding his fingers through hers, he lifted her hands above her head. Then he took his time, placing the tip of his cock at her entrance and sliding easily within, plunging every single inch into her in one hard stroke.

He pulled one hand away from hers to press down on her lower belly. "Feel me?"

"Yes."

Drake licked her lips before prying them open to devour her mouth in a passionate kiss as he began thrusting faster inside her. When he felt her tighten around him, he slowed, making her go slower as he gentled within her, riding until he felt her close to a climax, and then he went even slower.

Tilting her head back so he could look down into her face, he said, "I want to see your eyes when you come."

Bliss gazed up at him as he cupped her face in his hands, forcing her to look into his eyes while he finally set a rhythm that let the climax he had been teasing her with storm her body.

"That's it, sweet Bliss. Give it to me."

Drake drove his dick high within her, coming so hard he worried it was going to break the condom. Giving her lips a kiss, he lay down next to her, rubbing her back until she had almost fallen asleep in his arms. Then he rose up and untangled her arms from around his waist before going into the bathroom, where he washed off again then dried himself with the already-damp towel.

In the bedroom, Bliss rose up on her elbows as he passed the bed and went back out into the hallway. Gathering her pants and boots, he carried them back into the bedroom, picked up her top from the floor, and then dumped all her clothes on her naked body.

She stared at him in shocked surprise.

"Get dressed and get out."

The hurt expression on her face almost made him reconsider until he remembered how she had looked with Greer at Rosie's.

"You got what you wanted. I fucked you. The first time, I did it your way. The second was how I wanted to give it to you. You need to make up your mind which way you want it. The first way means you leave when it's over. The second means you stay the night and see where this goes, which means you're not running to fuck anyone with a dick when you're mad. When you decide, give me a call. Until then, I need to get some sleep. You wore me out. Oh, and lock the door behind you."

Drake went to the opposite side of the bed and climbed in. Yawning, he rolled onto his side, giving her his back. He waited for her to throw something at him or yell. Instead, he wasn't sure, but he thought he might have heard a small sniffle.

His hand clenched into a fist under his pillow. He wanted to drag her back to bed, but he had Porter blood in him, and Porters were born hunters. Drake was determined to catch the woman who wasn't even aware she was his prize.

Chapter Nine

"Would you like a cup of hot chocolate?"

"No, thanks," Bliss replied as she stared down at the book she was holding.

She heard Ginny go back into the kitchen as she continued to stare down sightlessly, her mind replaying the night before with Drake.

Picking up her cell phone, which was lying next to her on the sofa cushion, she saw that no calls or texts had come through. The other day when he had texted her, she had ignored them. Right then, however, she wished Drake would break and text her, relieving her of trying to make sense of her chaotic emotions.

Ginny came back into the room, carrying a mug, which she placed next to Bliss on the end table. "I brought it in case you changed your mind." Ginny then went to the closet and took out her coat.

"Thank you. You're going out?"

"I'm going to a movie with Willa and Lucky. Would you like to go?"

"No. I'm sure I'm the last person they want to see you show up with." Willa might have offered her a place to live, and Bliss believed she had truly forgiven her for breaking her grandmother's cookie jar during a bitch fit. However, Lucky, despite being a pastor, would abide by the club rules and maintain his distance.

Ginny pulled her hair out from under her coat. "I'm sure they wouldn't mind. Are you sure?"

"I'm sure. Have a good time."

"I will. I'll see you later."

"Bye."

Bliss stared at the closed door, wishing she could have gone, tired of staying inside the house. She needed to decide what her next step was going to be.

She had hated getting up to go to work early every morning. However, she needed to find a job, one that had a flexible schedule.

Bliss snorted to herself. As if a job like that existed. She didn't miss working in the factory, and even though they hadn't taken her job with the privileges of being a Last Rider, she had known it would be too hard to work there and watch their interactions from the outside.

She looked down at her silent cell phone again. Before she could change her mind, she called Drake.

"Hello."

"What are you doing?"

A brief silence met her question before he replied, "I'm about to take Jace and Cal for a ride."

"May I go?"

"Did you make up your mind?"

"Yes." Suddenly, the decision she had been struggling to make seemed clear. She had been fighting a losing battle. As much as she didn't want to admit it, she liked it when he treated her like what she thought and felt mattered. She couldn't remember if anyone ever had before.

"What's it going to be?"

"I want to do it your way."

"Can you be here in fifteen minutes?"

"Yes."

"I'll wait on you, then. Wear something warm."

"Okay." Bliss disconnected the call, jumping off the couch to run upstairs and change into a pair of jeans.

Searching through her drawers, she found a sweatshirt and tugged it on. She started to put on her leather boots, but instead, she went to her closet and took out a pair of suede ones with fur lining. It was cold outside, and flurries had started to fall.

Bliss wiggled her toes in the warm fur before running back downstairs to put on a coat. Her leather jacket was all she had, though; she would freeze her ass off. However, Ginny had a spare dark gray coat that was thicker. Bliss took it and slid it on. She didn't think Ginny would mind. Zipping it up, she then grabbed her purse.

She almost slid as she ran to her car in the driveway. Thankfully, not too much snow had accumulated on her windshield.

She was backing out of the driveway before the windshield wipers had made the first swipe, the car fishtailing slightly when she pressed down on the accelerator. Gripping the wheel tightly, she sped through the streets toward Drake's house. She was afraid if she took too long, he would leave without her.

She almost slid off the road when she made the turn into his driveway. Straightening the wheels, she managed to bring it to a stop in front of Drake's open garage.

Drake, Jace, and Cal all stood, watching her with open mouths before Drake stormed toward the car.

"Are you crazy going that fast on slick roads?" he asked in frustration when she got out.

"I didn't want you to leave without me."

A strange look came upon his face, his lips parting on a rough sigh.

He reached out his cold hand to cup her cheek. "Didn't you tell me you wanted to do things my way?"

Bliss nodded eagerly. Had he changed his mind, and he was going to let her down?

She looked down, unable to meet his eyes.

"In a relationship, couples wait for each other. I would have waited."

She glanced back up at him, giving a weak laugh. "I guess I'm used to The Last Riders. Whenever we went out, you had to get there before all the bikes were filled, or you got left behind."

Drake pointed to the garage. "No one else is riding next to me but you, either in my car or on my bike."

Bliss stared at the sports car he drove with the motorcycle sitting next to it in the garage.

"Okay." She gave him a trembling smile.

Jace and Cal were both busy talking and admiring the two other bikes sitting next to Drake's.

"You bought them motorcycles?"

"No, these are Rider's. For some reason they refuse to tell me, The Last Riders promised them motorcycles, despite the fact that they broke into the factory to look at said motorcycles. However, I put a stop to it. Thanks to the State of Kentucky, they needed my permission for their motorcycle licenses before they turned eighteen. Now that they're old enough to get their licenses, I want them to wait for their bikes until after graduation, and *I'll* be the one buying them, not The Last Riders.

"Since I'm not a complete hard-ass, I do occasionally let them go for a ride when they do something I'm proud of, like make an A on their Trigonometry test. Rider dropped them off about fifteen minutes ago."

"That's a definite incentive to get their grades up." Bliss stomped her feet to remain warm.

From the eagerness on the boys' faces, Drake might just be successful in getting them to walk up to the podium to get their diplomas.

Drake took her hand to lead her into the warm garage.

"Hi, Bliss."

"Hi, Jace, Cal. Cool bikes."

"Yes, they are!" Jace exclaimed. "Rider has some killer rides. You going for a ride with us?"

"You're still going to take them out? The roads are getting slick," she warned, seeing the snow was beginning to fall faster.

"I'd rather teach them how to ride on bad roads than have them learn by themselves when I'm not around. You ready?"

"Yes."

Drake got on his bike, straddling the monster with as much ease as any Last Rider. They wouldn't have hesitated to ride on a night like this, either.

Cal and Jace both mounted their borrowed motorcycles as she climbed on behind Drake.

"Ready?"

Bliss nodded against his shoulder.

"Jace, you and Cal go first. Ride next to each other. Go slow, and I'll follow behind."

The boys rode their bikes out of the garage as Drake started his motorcycle, riding behind them.

Bliss circled her arms around Drake's waist as they went, breathing in deeply. She had been afraid of riding with him, but that was before she realized how well he rode. Most weekenders were terrible, more show than skill. Drake definitely handled his motorcycle with skill.

She sucked in her breath when Cal's bike skidded, but the boy managed to straighten out.

"It's not the first time I've taken them out." Drake's calm voice had her relaxing against him.

Being on the back of a bike was like being out with an old friend. What was different was the man she was clinging to.

"You doing all right?"

"I'm fine." For the first time in a long time, Bliss believed she truly was.

Before, when she had ridden with someone else, she had felt carefree. Behind Drake, though, she felt safe and connected with the rider. It was different. She liked holding on to him. Plus, it was nice not having to worry about another woman grabbing her spot if they made a stop.

She didn't think she would be able to give up her spot behind Drake without a fight.

ꕤ

Drake leaned forward, skillfully guiding the wooden log out from underneath the others.

"Good move, Dad." Jace leaned forward to guide a piece out he had chosen. The wooden structure wobbled, but it didn't fall. It was her turn next.

Bliss wiped her sticky palms on the side of her pants. Carefully, she picked her log, sliding it out. The structure wobbled then steadied, and she blew out a breath of relief as she tugged it free.

"My turn." Cal's voice was overly confident in Bliss's opinion as he went for a log. The structure crumpled when it was only halfway out. "Dammit."

"You lose," Jace taunted.

Cal punched Jace in the shoulder. His friend didn't wince.

Drake stood, stretching. "Time for bed."

Bliss stacked the game pieces back into the box and straightened with the game in her hand as she felt Jace's arm wrap around her shoulder. The young man's mouth was headed toward her cheek when Drake smacked him against the back of his head.

"Okay, okay. You can't blame a guy for trying," Jace teased, releasing her.

"'Night, Drake, Bliss," Cal called as he headed to his room.

"Good night, boys."

Jace and Cal both winced in feigned pain as they went upstairs.

"That probably stung their pride a little."

"I call them as I see them."

Drake pressed against her back, his cock nestling against her behind as she leaned over to pick up the glasses sitting on the table.

Bliss shivered in anticipation. She knew what was behind that zipper and how good he was at using what God had gifted him with.

She edged reluctantly away from him, glancing upstairs. Carrying the glasses into the kitchen, she placed them in the sink. When she turned around, Drake was standing a few feet away from her. She could tell what he had in mind from the gleam in his eyes.

"It's time I went home."

"Why?"

"I feel weird with the boys here."

"Bliss, you wouldn't be the first woman to stay the night here with me."

She swallowed back the lump of hurt the remark made her acknowledge.

"It would be the first time I did, and I wouldn't feel right." She ran her hand through her short hair, realizing she hadn't gelled it into spikes before she had left her house.

"Jace and Cal are both over eighteen. The only reason they're still in high school is because Cal got behind when his mother became sick, and Jace got behind because he didn't want to graduate without Cal. They're attached at the hip. I didn't give Jace too much shit about it because I knew why he was acting up. They'll have enough credits to graduate in December but won't receive their diplomas until the end of the school year. They plan on entering the service next fall."

The thought of not seeing the boys around had Bliss feeling as if she already missed them. What in the hell was wrong with her? Why was she getting so attached to these males in such a short time?

"Which one are they planning on going into?"

"The Navy. I think Cash's stories helped make up their minds. Cash said he still has some contacts in the service, and he'll make sure they watch out for him."

Bliss could see the worry he couldn't hide.

"You can't change their minds?"

"I don't want to. Neither one of them wants to go to college. This town is dying. There aren't enough jobs in the area. The Last Riders are trying, but they can't employ the whole county. There are two smaller cities on the outskirts that have already died. In another twenty years, if something doesn't change, Treepoint won't be worth living in."

"It's not that bad," Bliss protested. Compared to some small towns she had ridden through on the back of a bike, Treepoint didn't have that deserted feeling.

"Yes, it is. I've lived here my whole life. It makes me sick to see what's happening here. Danny Owens is the mayor, and he's a piece of shit. He's letting the town fall apart. The fucking sidewalks are crumbling, and he's made no effort to fix them. Businesses that have dissolved are boarded up and falling down.

"The city council is even worse. It's filled with a bunch of people who are too old and stuck in their ways to change. I would bet the money in my checking account that most of them are filling their pockets with money from town projects that aren't being done.

"We used to have a huge truck that cleaned and washed the streets twice a week, but it broke down last year. A new one was supposed to be purchased. The council conveniently never brings it up in the meetings anymore. Dalton West is the senior member on the council. When I brought it up to him, he just said there wasn't enough money in the general fund."

"Elections are next year. Run for mayor." Even in the short time she had known Drake, she had learned he was strongly involved in the community. He was always attending some meeting about the school or government planning.

"I stand a snowball's chance in hell of winning an election in this town."

"Why? Everyone seems to like you." Bliss didn't think it would be as difficult as he believed. People came up to him constantly to say hi or to seek his advice when they were out.

"Because I wouldn't bend over to kiss ass in order to get votes."

"Maybe the town is ready for someone new. You won't know if you don't try," she urged.

"Even if I manage to win the mayoral election, nothing will change if I don't have allies on the city council."

"It will if you can convince others in town who are as concerned as you to run."

"There are three seats up for re-election. It would take all three to be on my side to force an outside audit and to get projects funded."

"You have a year to figure out who those people could be and convince them."

"You're a smart woman."

Bliss blushed at his compliment, moving to stand in front of him. "I better go before I change my mind." She rose up on her toes to try to reach his mouth yet couldn't quite make it.

His hands circled her waist, lifting her higher and meeting her halfway.

"I want you to change your mind."

She expected a passionate kiss; instead, she was overcome by a tenderness she had never dealt with before. There was something there she had never felt before either, but she wasn't sure what it was. She tried to put a name to the elusive emotion affecting her.

She wiggled until he placed her back on her feet.

"Drake, can I ask you a question?"

"Of course."

"Do you like me?"

"Of course."

Bliss shook her head at him, disappointed. She started past him but was stopped.

"What was that look for? I answered your question, but you don't look like you believe me."

"Because I don't. No one likes me." Why would he be any different than anyone else?

"That's not true. The Last Riders care about you. Jace, Cal, and I all do. Ask any woman in town I've been with. They'll all tell you that I haven't told them one lie when I was seeing them."

He wasn't making it better. Each word spilling from his lips was reinforcing the conclusion she had come to on her own: he was blowing smoke up her ass.

The Last Riders had tolerated her because she was always game for anything they wanted. Did she believe any of them liked her when they weren't humping her? Hell no. If she were to ask any member of the club what her favorite color was, not one male or female would be able to answer the question.

"The Last Riders don't care about me. They threw me out of the club. Jace, Cal, and you haven't known me long enough to know if you like me or not."

"Is that so?"

"Yes!" Bliss snapped. "I'm no different than any other woman you've fucked in town."

Drake burst into laughter.

"Are you laughing at me?" Hurt, she tried to leave again.

"Bliss, I was the one trying to take time to get to know you better. You're the one who was determined to keep everything on a physical level. Let me remind you that I have made it perfectly clear to you that I want to have a relationship with you, which is what I thought you were agreeing with when you called. Now you're getting angry at me because I told you I care about you?"

Bliss had to admit she might have overreacted and was deathly afraid to admit why.

"I need to leave."

Drake easily lifted her so he could look into her eyes.

"What's wrong?" That time, his question was a demand.

"I think I like you, too." She was frightened to reveal her feelings out loud, both to herself and Drake. Men liked the chase, losing interest once they had achieved their goal.

She liked that he asked her first what she wanted to eat when they went out. She liked that he didn't look at other women when they went out, rode a bike, and damn, she really liked the way he treated her as if she had the cleanest reputation in town. Most of all, she really liked the way he kissed her.

She kept expecting him to become bored and make an excuse to leave. She dreaded the thought that each time she saw him would be the last. It was like standing on a railroad track, waiting for a train to hit you.

His expression gentled. "And that's bad?"

"Time will tell."

She wasn't a schoolgirl who believed in sweet endings. She was a grown woman who had watched others win the men in her life.

Could she handle letting another man she cared about move on to another woman when he tired of her? As always, she was going to take the ride and hope for the best. She was going to take the risk that Drake was being straight with her. What did she have to lose at this point?

The tiny little seed of hope that wanted to believe that someone could love her.

Chapter Ten

Here. Now.

Bliss smiled at the text message on her phone then asked Ginny, "Can we finish this later?"

Ginny opened another tub of ornaments they had carried down from Willa's attic. Willa had come by and picked up several boxes of Christmas decorations earlier, telling them they were welcome to use the rest.

"Sure," she said. "I need to get back to work anyway. We can decorate the tree tonight, if you're not busy with Drake."

"He's having dinner with a friend of Cash's tonight. The boys are going along, too. Drake wants them to know what they're getting into before they sign on the dotted lines." She had made the suggestion to Drake. Having listened to too many horror stories of the men in the club, she felt the boys needed to know how their lives would change. The boys who left Treepoint would not be the same two coming back.

It had shocked her when Drake had taken her advice and called Cash, asking him if he knew someone who would give the boys the real facts of joining the service. Cash had set the meeting up with a friend who was willing to drive in from Ohio, where he was on leave.

"Are they getting nervous?

"No, but Drake is. I think his supportive parenting view is slipping. I don't blame him. I just wish they would at least do a semester of college before they decide." She had grown attached to the two boys in the short time she and Drake had spent together.

During Thanksgiving, she had thought she would miss being with The Last Riders. She had, but it had been in a melancholy way, not the heartbreaking way she had been dealing with since she had left.

Bliss went to the closet, taking out her jacket.

"Take mine. That one isn't warm enough."

Bliss put hers back on the hanger, taking Ginny's spare winter coat.

"Why don't you buy yourself a thicker coat? That one's too big for you."

"Why should I spend the money when I can borrow yours?" Bliss quipped.

Ginny never complained about her making the spare coat her own since she had purchased a newer one for herself when she had gone shopping for Willa's thank-you gift.

The awkwardness of the first few months they had lived together was gone. Since then, they talked more easily and had begun watching her favorite show, *Vikings,* together. Each of them picked their TV boyfriends. Surprisingly, it was Ginny who kept their conversations from reaching a personal level.

"That's true. I can't argue with common sense. See you later."

"Bye." Bliss rushed out, not wanting to keep Drake waiting. At least the roads were cleared. The city council's penny-pinching hadn't extended to snow removal yet.

Drake's car was the only one outside his office building when she parked.

As she walked on the sidewalk toward his office, she noticed what Drake had been concerned about. The town was beginning to look neglected. The sheriff's office and Lucky's church were the only two buildings that had fronts appearing cleaned and cared for. Even the diner looked like it could use a fresh coat of paint.

Bliss didn't knock before entering Drake's office where she simply stood, trying to catch her breath. Whenever she looked at him, it made breathing difficult. She had always been drawn to strong men, and Drake's size and confidence aroused her on an elemental level that grew each time she was with him.

"What took you so long?" Drake was sitting behind his desk, wearing a dark suit with a dark gray shirt.

Bliss frowned, glancing at the clock on his desk.

"I was joking." The irritation on his face and in his voice disappeared. In its place was an expression that came damn close to the one her favorite TV boyfriend had perfected.

"Oh."

"Come here." Drake leaned back in his leather chair.

She unbuttoned the heavy coat as she walked around the corner of his desk. When she stepped within reach, he leaned forward, using the front sides of the coat to tug her down onto his lap.

"You have no sense of humor."

"I didn't think it was funny," she told him, lowering her lashes so he couldn't see the hurt in her eyes. She used to love to play the same game with Shade and had been thrilled when he would punish her for taking too long. Many times, she would be the instigator so she would get the attention she wanted from him. From Drake, though, she kept waiting for the train to hit. Some days, she swore she could almost hear it coming, as if fate was bearing down on her to pay her back for being such a bad person.

"Sweet Bliss, what am I going to do with you?"

"Do you need me to make some suggestions?" she teased, shrugging off her feelings as unimportant as her lips went to the corner of his mouth, her fingers playing with his belt buckle.

Drake brought his hand to her hair, holding her in place as his mouth captured hers and took the kiss she was being stingy with. His tongue wrapped around hers before sucking it into his mouth.

She fucking loved the way he tasted, like a dark, rich brandy and something else that had her lifting her head in surprise.

"Have your cousins been in for a visit?"

"Greer needed a favor, and he always brings his best when he's bargaining."

Bliss went to her knees between his thighs. "Did you save me any?"

"I might have one or two in my desk, but I wouldn't be part Porter if I didn't make you bargain for it."

Bliss unbuckled his belt. "I think I might have something you would be willing to bargain for." Reverently, she pulled his already-thick cock out of his pants.

Leaning over, she licked the broad tip, and Drake sucked in a deep breath as his ass came slightly off the chair.

Bliss rolled her tongue around the tip, wondering how in the hell she was ever going to fit him in her mouth.

She scooted closer on her knees as she stroked his cock with a soft touch while her mouth circled the head. His hand went to the back of her neck as she sucked him into the warmth of her mouth.

"Why do you wear so much hair spray?" He stroked her neck, making goose bumps rise on her flesh.

Bliss lifted her head so she could answer him. "I like knowing it will stay in place."

"It's definitely not going anywhere. You should let your hair grow out some. You would look hot as fuck with longer hair."

She flicked her tongue against the slit of his dick. "You don't think I'm hot now?"

A groan was her only answer.

Bliss used her tongue to give her hand enough moisture to slide slickly up and down his huge cock. Rubbing her breasts against his leg, she used every bit of the skills she had acquired from living with The Last Riders to wreck the control Drake never lost.

He kept his hand on her neck, making her hornier the more she sucked on him. She tried to take more yet couldn't.

"Stop trying to take more than you can. The head is the most sensitive part, anyway."

Bliss wanted to groan in frustration. Not many women would have tried to take more than the head, but she was determined to outdo any woman before her.

Relaxing her throat and breathing through her nose, she scooted even closer so she could change her angle. A surge of pride went through her when she felt him slide deeper in her mouth, reaching her throat.

"Son of a bitch!"

She wanted to grin when she felt him make himself still so he wouldn't hurt her.

Gliding her hand down, she found his balls and squeezed them both. At the same time, she forced herself to swallow, tightening her throat around his thick cock. A second later, his balls tightened as she felt the first taste of his climax.

When he was finished, she raised her head, giving the slit a last flick.

The dumbfounded expression on his face had her giggling.

"I take it you liked it?"

Drake opened his desk drawer, taking out a baggie with three joints. "I'm not even going to make you share."

ꙮ

Bliss pushed the star with the revolving Santa sleigh down carefully on the top of the tree. It was so old and delicate she was afraid it was going to break.

Climbing down the ladder, she picked up the cord at the bottom of the tree. All the lights blinked then went out before coming back on in a twinkling rhythm.

"It's beautiful, isn't it?"

Ginny placed the last ornament before stepping back to view the tree they had been working on for several hours. "It's the prettiest I've ever had."

"Me, too," Bliss agreed. "Want some hot chocolate?"

"That sounds really good right now. I'll make it." Ginny used the toe of her tennis shoe to scoot an empty box out of the way.

"I will. You made the last cup. It's my turn."

"Okay, I'll clean up in here, then." Ginny began throwing the discarded bits and pieces of decorations they hadn't used into the empty box.

Bliss went into the kitchen, humming "Jingle Bells." There were three weeks until Christmas, but the snow outside and decorating the tree had put her in a festive mood.

The hot chocolate was almost done when she heard the doorbell. She assumed it was someone for Ginny since no one except Drake ever came by for her, and he, Jace, and Cal were having dinner with the Navy guy.

She fixed an extra mug in case Ginny wanted to offer one to her guest. Then, carrying them carefully into the other room, she kept her eyes cast down so she wouldn't spill any of the hot liquid.

She froze when she glanced up after coming through the kitchen doorway.

"There she is now. How have you been, Bliss?"

Bliss's fingers trembled. She didn't feel the hot liquid scalding her fingers or care that it dripped to the carpet they had just cleaned for the holidays. Her attention was focused on the man sprawled comfortably on the couch, making himself at home.

She had to clear her throat a couple of times to force the strangled greeting out.

"Hi, Stark."

Chapter Eleven

"You're burning yourself!" Ginny jumped up from the couch where she had been sitting next to the biker Bliss had hoped never to see again. She took two of the cups, gingerly handing one to Stark then setting hers on the end table. "I'll get some paper towels and an ice pack for your hand."

Bliss didn't try to stop her.

Moving farther into the room, she sat down on the chair across from the couch, setting her mug on the coffee table.

"Why are you here?"

"To see you, of course. I heard you're not with The Last Riders anymore. That true?"

Bliss wildly thought about lying for a brief second, but she knew he wouldn't be there if he wasn't already sure of his facts. "Yes."

She wanted to scream. She was nailing her own coffin closed.

The grin on his smug face confirmed the fears churning in her stomach.

Before either of them could say anything else, Ginny came back into the room, handing her some ice.

Bliss carefully wiped her sticky hand off before placing the ice pack on the angry red burn.

"Are you okay?"

"Yes," Bliss lied. She needed to get Ginny out of the room before Stark showed his true colors. "If you're still in the mood, do you mind running to the diner and picking up some burgers?"

"All right. Would you like me to get you one, Stark?"

"No!" Bliss forced herself to calm her panicked voice. The last thing she wanted was to alert Ginny that something was wrong, or Stark wouldn't let her leave. "He told me he can't stay long."

"That's a shame. He told me while you were in the kitchen that you're old friends."

Bliss wouldn't call what she and Stark had shared a friendship.

"I'll be right back," she promised, picking up her purse.

"Take your time." Bliss gave her the only warning she could without making it obvious.

Stark coldly watched the two of them with calculating eyes, and she tensed. If he so much as made a move to try to stop Ginny, she would throw the mug of cocoa at him, giving the other woman enough time to hopefully get out the door.

He sat still, a smirk on his mouth as if he could read her mind.

She didn't break eye contact with him until she heard the door close behind Ginny.

"You afraid I'll hurt her?"

"I know you would."

He shook his head at her. "You're still the same stupid bitch you always were. You should know I do my homework better than that. She works for The Last Riders. Best friends with Lucky's wife."

He *had* done his homework. The only thing that had kept her safe from the Devil's Rejects had been their fear of The Last Riders. Ginny fell under the protection of the club, while hers had been withdrawn. She was a sitting duck.

She should have run as soon as the club had thrown her out; however, she hadn't been able to bear the thought of being away from them without even the possibility of catching glimpses of them. She had also hoped she had been with The Last Riders long enough that Stark would have lost interest and quit checking up on her. That weakness was going to cost her the very freedom she had gained when The Last Riders had helped her escape from Stark in the first place.

"What do you want?"

"What do you think? I'm going to make it a no-brainer for you. I'll give you five minutes to grab what you want to take with you. If that sexy bitch comes back before we're out of here, both of you will be leaving with me."

Bliss didn't doubt him for a second. She was sure he wouldn't have shown up at her front door without backup waiting outside.

To Stark, she was a possession, like his boots and bike. He had told her one time, when she had come to after one of his chokeholds, that she would never get away from him.

"If you die, bitch, I'll burn your fucking body and keep your ashes on my bedside table. When I die, the brothers will bury your ashes with me. You've been mine since you were fifteen, and you'll fucking die that way."

Bliss stood, going to the steps. She wouldn't take a chance with Ginny's safety. Hell was waiting for the young woman if Bliss didn't follow his order.

Her foot was on the first step when the doorbell rang. Thinking it was one of Stark's men, she answered the door to find Drake on the doorstep.

Bliss paled. Her nightmare had just become worse, if that was possible.

Using her body to shield Stark from Drake's view, she held the door with a death grip to prevent him from entering.

"I thought I would stop by and see if you wanted to watch a movie."

"Not tonight. I'm kind of busy."

"Doing what?"

Bliss's mind went blank, and she became angry that her life was such an empty shell that it was going to get Drake killed. She tried a different tactic.

"I have company. I'll see you tomorrow," she said, knowing Stark was going to make sure she never stepped foot back in Treepoint again.

"Who?" Drake's expression didn't change; it was just as affable as when she had answered the door.

Bliss heard Stark coming up behind her, and then the door was jerked from her grasp.

"Me, motherfucker. You need to step away while you still have the chance before me and my friends stomp the living shit out of you."

Bliss pressed a hand to Stark's chest. "It's okay, Stark. Drake is leaving." She turned pleadingly to Drake. "You better go."

Before she could blink, Drake shoved her back into the house, and Stark was thrust against the door with a gun pressed to the side of his head.

Bliss stood, openmouthed, as two bikers jumped off their motorcycles and ran forward. Drake didn't take his eyes off Stark.

"You better call them off before Bliss has to have her door repainted, because no soap and water is going to wash away the brains I'm about to splatter all over it."

"Get back, Cracker, Whip. Go back to the bikes."

Bliss watched as the dangerous bikers pulled up short then began backing away when they saw a gun pressed to their leader's skull.

"They leave?" Drake snapped out.

"Yes, they went back to their bikes."

"Call Knox and tell him to get his ass over here."

"I don't have to. He's pulling into the driveway." Bliss wrapped her arms around her stomach, shivering from the cold air coming through the open door.

"Ginny must have called him after she called me." Drake was pressing the gun against Stark's head so hard the ruddy flesh was becoming white.

Her roommate hadn't been as clueless as Bliss had believed.

"You have a permit for that gun, Drake?" The stony face of the largest Last Rider, serving as sheriff, didn't betray the many intimate moments they had shared.

"I've had my concealed and carry since it became legal." Drake didn't move the gun away from Stark, holding it steady as Knox drew closer. His deputies surrounded the group of men sitting on their motorcycles.

"Put it away. You might have a license to carry it, but that doesn't mean you know how to use it."

"I know how to use it better than any of those deputies standing over there with their hands in their pockets."

"They don't need to pull their guns on them. The only one posing a threat right now is you."

Drake moved the gun away from Stark, placing it back in his waistband.

"You don't keep it in a holster?"

"No, the second it takes you to pull it free gives who you're aiming for another second of breath."

"Holsters keep you from blowing your dick off."

"My gun doesn't go off by mistake," Drake promised as Stark straightened from the door, throwing him a venomous glare.

"Want to tell me why you were aiming it at Stark?"

"You know this piece of shit?" Drake gave Knox an incredulous look.

"Unfortunately," Knox admitted, casually placing his body between the two men.

"I want him put in jail for attacking me!" Stark yelled.

Bliss would have laughed at the look Drake was giving Stark, which was the same one he had given Knox, but she didn't think he would find the humor in the situation.

Drake raised his gun at Stark again, but Knox reached out, making him lower it again.

"You attack him, Drake?"

"Yes, he's trespassing," Drake ground out, glaring at Stark as if he was still thinking of shooting him.

"I was invited inside," Stark snarled.

"That true, Bliss?" Knox questioned.

Bliss found herself the focus of the men. Drake's concern was obvious, while Knox was impassive, waiting for her answer. Stark was threatening, giving her a silent warning to watch her choice of words.

"No. He told Ginny we were old friends, and she let him inside."

"We are friends."

"We were never friends, Stark." Forcing her gaze to remain on Knox, she felt the menace coming off Stark in waves. "He was trying to make me leave with him, and he threatened Ginny's freedom." Bliss hoped Stark's threat toward Ginny would rouse Knox to make sure she was safe from the biker lowlife. Knox would make no effort to protect her. However, if he saw to it that The Last Riders took care of Stark to ensure Ginny's safety, then it assured hers, as well.

"You didn't want to go with him?"

"No, I didn't want to go with him," Bliss snapped, her hands clenched at her sides. Knox knew damn well what life would hold for her if Stark had her in his possession again.

She forced back the hurt feelings of his uncaring attitude. They'd had sex more times than she could remember before he had married Diamond. Her loyalty to the men had been unquestionable—it was the women they had chosen that she couldn't accept. She would have died rather than betray any of The Last Riders, yet Knox was standing there as if he couldn't have cared less that Stark would have made her life a living hell.

The hurt feelings were useless and weak. She wasn't the same woman the Devil's Rejects had kept under their control. It was time Stark realized she wasn't going to be his victim any longer.

"I want him arrested."

"What for?"

"Attempted kidnapping."

Knox motioned to his deputy to come and take Stark. When the deputy had placed the biker in the back of Knox's squad car, he turned back to her.

"I already planned on arresting him, but the charge isn't going to hold long. When it goes to court, both of us know what's going to come out of his mouth. It's going to be your word against his. Did he threaten you and Ginny in front of her or Drake?"

"No," Bliss reluctantly admitted.

Drake placed a supportive arm around her shoulder.

"Come to my office in the morning and get a restraining order. You'll stand a better chance of that succeeding."

"Okay."

Knox took her and Drake's statements. Ginny came back and described what had taken place, learning the details of what had happened after she had left.

"I'm so angry at myself. I shouldn't have opened the door. I know better than that. I could have been responsible for you being kidnapped."

Bliss shook her head, not wanting Ginny to feel responsible. "If you hadn't let him in, he would have caught me when I was leaving or just broken in after we were both asleep. You called Drake and the police. You saved me, Ginny." Bliss gave her hand a grateful squeeze.

Knox didn't take long to finish his report. "I'll see you in the morning."

"Good night." Bliss had started to close the door behind him as Ginny went into the kitchen to make coffee when Knox turned back around.

"You know a restraining order isn't going to stop him. It's going to make him angrier," he warned. "I want you to get the order, don't get me wrong, but a smart woman would make damn sure she knew what she was going to do if Stark decides he wants to break it. Buy yourself a gun or borrow Drake's. Hell, move in with Drake. Do what you have to do to keep yourself safe."

"I'll be gone before he makes bail."

"You're not going anywhere." Drake wrapped an arm around her waist, pulling her back against him. "'Night, Knox."

"'Night, Bliss, Drake."

Bliss couldn't bring herself to face Drake, standing still in his arms as he leaned forward to shut the door. She was ashamed that he'd found out she had once been involved with Stark.

"You okay?"

"Hold me tighter."

His arms tightened around her waist, surrounding her in his warmth.

Neither turned when Ginny came back in the room.

"I set your coffee cups on the side table. I'll leave you alone to talk."

"Thank you again, Ginny."

Her soft "You're welcome" floated down the stairs.

"You're not leaving town," Drake declared.

Bliss stared sightlessly at the door. She wasn't about to let her past destroy a man she had begun to care about. Not only could Drake get hurt, but Stark was dirty enough not to care who else was harmed in the process. Jace, Cal, and Ginny would mean nothing to Stark. He wouldn't hesitate to use them to keep Drake in line.

"I can't stay. I couldn't bear it if you were hurt. You're not capable of dealing with Stark and his club. The Devil's Rejects aren't like The Last Riders. They're evil, and I'm certainly not worth getting someone killed over."

"Don't say that!"

"It's the truth." Bliss gave a bitter laugh. "I'm a club whore. I've fucked every member of the Devil's Rejects and The Last Riders. There hasn't been anything or anyone I haven't done. Is that the kind of woman you want in your life? Around your son?"

Drake buried his mouth in her nape. "Jace cares about you, Bliss. I do, too."

Bliss reinforced the guards she had placed on her heart years before. "There's no pussy worth dying for. I'm good, but I'm not that good."

"Stop before I spank your ass for talking about yourself like that! Stark won't hurt you or anyone else. I'll make sure of that."

"Stark doesn't play fair. He thinks I'm his. My mother was a club whore Stark used to control me. He raped me when I was fifteen and was sharing me by the time I was seventeen. I can't have children because they used me so hard one night that I spent a week in the hospital. I couldn't press charges or leave, because my mom refused to go with me, and I wasn't going to leave her behind.

"After she died, I tried to leave twice. Both times, he almost killed me. I stopped trying to leave when my brothers came looking for me. Stark let them leave alive, but he told me that if they came back he would kill them. He gave me his word he would leave them alone if they stayed away.

"I called them on the phone they gave me and told them I wasn't interested in getting the family back together." Bliss gave a bitter smile. "I could tell they were relieved. I didn't look my best when they came in, could see they were disgusted. They thought I was just like our mother. And I was by that time. I didn't care who or how I did the men in the club. I was just trying to survive one day after another.

"You want to know something weird?" she continued.

"What?" Drake croaked out.

"I don't know why I tried so hard to survive. I thought I deserved everything they did to me because I must have been bad. I hadn't taken good enough care of my mother, couldn't make her love me more than the drugs, hadn't been smart in school.

"If I made it through the day without getting smacked around, I thought it was a good day. The nights were the worst, though. That's when I had to sleep with that disgusting bastard. He's evil. The club used to joke that Stark always escaped being killed because the devil didn't even want him.

"I would still be there if it wasn't for The Last Riders. The Devil's Rejects bit off more than they could chew when they started a war with them. They stole some of the men's bikes and a woman member when the club was out on a ride. Viper retaliated by striking back at their clubhouse. The difference was The Last Riders attacked while the club was there.

"I still remember that night. I watched as every man in the club was killed or hurt badly enough to wish he was dead. The only reason Stark lived was because Viper wanted to humiliate him for not being a strong enough leader to protect his men.

"Viper offered the women a place with The Last Riders if they wanted to leave. Five of us chose to go. Viper helped us back on our feet. None of us had willingly wanted to be with the Devil's Rejects. Three of them found jobs and moved on. A fourth ended up marrying one of Viper's men, and they left the club."

"You stayed."

"I stayed. I knew Stark would find me—he had before. Viper offered to help me find a place, to help me find my brothers." Bliss's eyes darkened in pain. "Viper found out Stark hadn't kept his word to me. He had killed them a month after I had called them. He wanted to make sure I wouldn't try to run to them.

"Stark was never a man of his word, but Viper was. He asked me if I wanted him to find me another place to live, but I told him no. I liked The Last Riders. I felt safe. I wasn't ready to give that up.

"He wouldn't let the men touch me for a year, said I needed time to get my head on straight and figure out what I wanted."

"Which was?"

"To be one of them. They're loyal and fierce, Drake. They would die to protect each other. I wanted that for myself."

"Bliss…"

"A woman can become a member by fucking or making six out of the eight original members come. One night, I walked up to Rider and sucked his dick off in front of Train. They were my first two votes."

"Sweet Bliss…"

"Please, don't call me that…Please, don't. I'm not sweet. I don't know how to be. That's why they threw me out. I was too mean to the women. I couldn't be friendly with the women who were taking the men away from the club.

"If they didn't want to have sex with me, then why would they protect me? I needed their protection. I still do. That's why

I wanted Shade so badly. If I could have made him care, he would have made sure Stark never came near me again. I can't go back to the Devil's Rejects."

"You don't need The Last Riders anymore, especially not Shade." Drake forced her to turn around and face him. "I can protect you. Trust me."

He would never understand what he was asking of her. He wanted her to stand still with the train roaring right at her and not try to jump out of the way. She had trusted Stark twice, and he had nearly destroyed her. She had trusted she would always be a Last Rider, and that had ended.

Bliss laid her head on his chest. "I'll try."

"I won't let you down."

She had faced fears many times in her life, but never had she felt the terror clutching at her heart. Trust didn't come easily to her. She could count on one hand the number of people she had trusted during her lifetime, and they had all failed her. Bliss didn't think she would survive if she was disappointed again.

Chapter Twelve

"That wasn't so bad, was it?"

"I guess not."

No restraining order was going to make Stark stay away from her, but Bliss had decided to place her fragile trust in Drake for the time being. The only reason she hadn't already disappeared was because of the man walking confidently by her side.

"Where you going now?"

Bliss shrugged. "I was just going to head back to the house."

"I promised Cal I would take him to see his little sister this morning. Want to come?" he asked, before explaining, "With Cal's father serving prison time, the courts thought it would be psychologically damaging to deny her seeing Cal. Her foster mother takes her to daycare for a few hours a day so she can play with other children her age and to give Cal a place to visit Darcy. She doesn't feel comfortable with him coming to her home. It won't take long. Then, if you want, we could have Jace bring a pizza home when he gets off work and watch a movie."

"It's better than what I had planned." She really didn't want to go home by herself. Stark was still sitting in his jail cell, but she knew she would just worry if she was alone.

Drake opened his car door for her, and Bliss wearily climbed inside.

He cast her a glance as he started the car. "You look tired."

"I didn't sleep well."

"Afraid one of the Devil's Rejects would come for you?"

"Yes." Bliss rested her head on the window. Every sound in the house had her sitting up in bed, listening. She had fallen asleep near dawn with her cell phone in her hand and 911 keyed in so all she would have to do was hit the call button.

Drake squeezed her knee. "Don't worry, no one's going to interrupt your dreams but me."

"I dreamed about you when I finally fell asleep," Bliss admitted.

"Do you know that, when you dream about a person, it's because they were thinking about you?"

Bliss smiled. "Were you?"

"Yes. I've been thinking about you a lot, actually."

"What about?"

"About how good it feels when you're sucking my dick."

Bliss felt her mood lightening. "You're a jerk."

"A horny jerk. When are you going to break and spend the night with me or let me spend the night with you?"

"When Jace and Cal leave to join the service or Ginny spends the night away. I told you I don't feel comfortable with Jace and Cal there, and I know Ginny wouldn't at my place."

"So, we're going to keep fucking at my office and the hotel?"

"Look at it this way, it adds excitement."

"Having you in my bed all night would be exciting enough."

Bliss covered his hand on her knee with hers as they pulled into the driveway of his house. A minute later, Cal came out to squeeze into the back seat.

"Thanks for taking me, Drake."

Cal and Jace had gone in together to buy themselves a car to share, but Jace ended up with it most of the time since his job was delivering pizzas. And right then, Jace had the car.

"No problem."

Drake drove back to town, parking on the street a block down from Main Street. The daycare had opened a few months back in the building next to the one that held Diamond's office.

Drake got out, and then Cal climbed out on his side. Bliss remained sitting.

"You coming?"

"I thought I would wait here."

"Come on, he's going to be at least thirty minutes."

Sighing, Bliss got out, coming around the front of the car. "I like what they've done to the building." The front of the old building had been painted a pretty shade of bright yellow. "Happy Friends" was printed boldly across the door.

"I do, too."

Bliss went in after Drake to see a woman ushering Cal into a large room where several children of different ages were playing.

"Are you sure it's okay we're here?"

"I'm sure. Cal has the court's permission to see Darcy for two hours a week. He tries to come by and see her every day before he goes to work at the grocery store. I know the owner. Jessie Hayes opened it last month. She bought the building from me and knows I'm Cal's guardian until he graduates."

Bliss unobtrusively studied the woman. She had brown hair and was dressed in jeans and a sweatshirt that had Santa on it as she went to the little girl sitting by herself at a table, sucking her thumb and holding a small, worn blanket on her lap.

The little girl's face didn't light up when her brother crouched down next to her.

"Hi, Darcy. How's my baby sister doing?"

Bliss winced at the sound of Cal's voice. The sight of Darcy sitting off by herself had affected him.

She had missed her brothers when they had been taken away, and Bliss wondered how her life would have turned out if she had been able to stay in contact with them. Maybe she would have never met Stark, or maybe her brothers would have been killed even earlier.

She was glad the sad child had her brother. It was obvious Cal loved his little sister as he ruffled her hair, trying to bring a smile to her face.

Bliss and Drake sat down on a couple of chairs that had been placed against the wall while the children all watched them curiously as Cal picked a book to read to his sister.

One brave, blue-eyed little boy wandered closer. "What's your name?"

Bliss felt uncomfortable for a second, waiting for the daycare owner to rush the child away from her. "Bliss. What's yours?"

"I'm not allowed to talk to strangers."

Bliss didn't mention the fact that he had been the one to approach her.

"Want a carrot stick? I have some left over from snack time. I don't like carrots."

She tried to keep a solemn face as the little boy took out three carrot sticks from his jeans pocket. Bliss didn't want to hurt his feelings, but there was no way she was going to eat one of the unappetizing sticks nestled in the palm of his hand.

"No, thanks. I don't like carrots, either. I think Drake likes them, though." Bliss raised a brow, trying to keep from laughing.

"I'm not hungry. I had my snack before I came here."

"You sure?" The boy's face fell.

It didn't affect Drake. "I'm sure."

"Come back to the group, Devon. You're missing the best part of the story." Jessie came up from behind the boy to lead him back to the group.

Bliss had tensed, expecting her to ask her not to talk to the children. She was floored when she was given a friendly smile instead.

"He's adorable," Bliss remarked, relaxing back on her chair.

"I think he knows it, too," Drake remarked. "I'm going to have some serious competition in a few years."

Bliss didn't think so. Drake would be hard to beat, even though she wouldn't use the word "adorable" to describe him.

Bliss watched as Jessie read to the small group that had gathered around her. When she finished, the children played around the room in different areas. Jessie then came to stand next to their chairs, keeping a watchful eye on the children while speaking to Bliss.

"Hi. I'm Jessie." She held out her hand, which Bliss shook as she introduced herself.

"You've gotten another child since the last time I was here," Drake commented.

"I'm at full capacity until I can hire another worker."

"That shouldn't be too hard."

"You would think so, but the women applying for the position aren't passing their drug tests, or they have a police record. I have three children on a waiting list, and I can't take them until I find someone."

"If I think of anyone who might be interested, I'll let you know."

"I would appreciate it. One mother is going to lose her job if she doesn't find someone soon. Her last babysitter moved away."

"I could help out until you find someone you want to hire permanently." Bliss wanted to take the words back immediately. There was no way this woman wouldn't realize she used to belong to The Last Riders. While the outfit she was wearing wasn't as sexually suggestive as most of the clothes she usually wore, it didn't scream babysitter, either.

Jessie's face became ecstatic, however. "That would help out a lot. Do you have any experience with children in a preschool?"

"No."

"Do you at least like children?"

"Yes."

"Right now, I'll take that. I don't mean to be personal, but to save us both some time, will you pass the drug test?"

"Yes."

Bliss felt Drake's sharp glance. He had given her the joints, but she hadn't smoked them. She had taken them to keep him from smoking them. She didn't like the taste of them and hadn't wanted to tell him that.

"Do you have a police record?"

"No," Bliss lied. Shade had made sure her juvenile record had been destroyed. However, none of those charges would endanger the children; they would only embarrass her.

"You're hired...pending your drug test and the police record coming back clean. I'll get you an application." Jessie went to the desk in the corner and pulled out some papers, bringing them back to her with a pen. "If you want, you can do them now, and I can get everything started. It should only take a couple of days if you stop by the hospital when you leave here for the drug test."

"That's fine." Bliss took the papers and pen from Jessie.

What in the hell was she doing? She was going to have to leave when Stark came back after her, so why was she tying herself to this town?

Jessie went to break up two girls squabbling over a doll while Bliss began filling out the paperwork to avoid Drake's curious eyes.

"You sure about this?"

"No, but I'll stick with it until she hires someone else. It'll give me something to do besides fuck you when you're bored during the day."

"I hope she finds someone to replace you soon."

"Me, too," Bliss said fervently.

Chapter Thirteen

"Do angels fly?" Devon asked as Bliss wiped the glue off his small hands.

"Some do." Bliss picked up the picture of an angel he had been coloring. It was soggy because he had used so much glue to apply glitter to the wings. "If they've earned their wings."

"How do you become an angel?" Devon tagged along behind her as she pinned his picture to the wall.

Bliss took her time answering the delicate question.

"My mama's an angel." Darcy wobbled over to the picture, pointing to the one she had colored with blue hair. Her blue-green eyes filled with tears, a contrast to her expensive, festive dress with little Christmas trees and her long, blondish-brown hair that was braided and had a big red bow at the end.

Bliss leaned over, picking the child up into her arms. Despite herself, Bliss was becoming attached to the motherless little girl.

Jessie had told her Darcy had been placed in a foster home when her mother had passed away and Cal's father had been sent to prison. Bliss didn't tell her that she already knew, not wanting to bring up her connection to The Last Riders until she had to. She really liked working with the children, and she didn't even mind getting out of bed in the morning to rush there. Surprisingly, she had also asked Ginny to go to the department store with her to pick out more appropriate clothes.

Bliss didn't care for the woman taking care of Darcy. Lisa West was a bitch; Bliss was an expert at recognizing them, because she was one.

"How did she become an angel?" Devon asked Darcy.

"Jesus missed her, so he took her home. I miss her, too. Do you think he would bring her back if I asked Santa?"

Bliss considered her heart unbreakable, but Darcy was putting a crack in it. A big one.

"Sweetheart, I don't think Santa can do that. Santa brings presents to good little boys and girls."

"I've been reeeal good."

"I have, too!" Dalton chimed in.

"Not as good as me." Darcy was crying with big, fat tears rolling down her cheeks.

Bliss carried her to the reading corner where Jessie had placed a rocking chair. Sitting down with the girl on her lap, Bliss began humming a song she had thought she had long forgotten.

Darcy's chubby hand reached out to grasp her blanket, brushing the satin ribbon at the end against her wet cheek.

"What's the name of that song? It's pretty."

"'Hush Little Baby,'" Bliss choked out.

"I like it."

"I do, too. My mama used to sing it to me when I was little."

Darcy's head fell to her breast as Bliss slowly rocked the chair and hummed. Her lids lowered, and her breathing evened out as she fell asleep.

Jessie had laid out the napping cots, so Bliss carried the girl to the one closest to the desk. That way, she could watch over Darcy as she napped. She covered her with a blanket Jessie handed her, and then Bliss helped Jessie lay the rest of the children down. Most of them fell asleep as soon as they lay down, while the rest wiggled before settling down and drifting off.

"She's a sweet kid," Jessie remarked, throwing herself down in the chair behind the desk.

"Yes, she is," Bliss replied as she went around the room, picking up the toys and straightening the learning centers.

Jessie sat at her desk, watching her as she ate her lunch. "You're very good with children," she complimented.

"I like them. I always have. I would babysit a friend of mine's twins whenever they let me."

"They *let* you?"

"I had to stand in line. They had several friends volunteering."

"Oh. Sit down and take a break." Jessie pulled out the chair next to hers then handed Bliss a sandwich. "I made extra. I noticed you have a habit of not eating lunch."

"I'm not a very good cook."

"I'm going to give you a secret recipe with only three ingredients."

Bliss unwrapped the sandwich, taking a bite of the gooey goodness.

"Bread, peanut butter, and jelly."

"I can add another recipe to my file. Microwavable macaroni and cheese, cups of soup, and now peanut butter and jelly sandwiches." Bliss chewed the sandwich, expecting to be assailed by bad memories of the many times she had eaten them when she was a child. It was a staple at homeless shelters.

When she had been living with the Devil's Rejects, it was often the only thing she could scrounge together for a meal. After she had been rescued, she had sworn never to eat one again. Some things in life were inevitable, though, and peanut butter and jelly was one of them.

"Keep it up and you'll become as good as me."

"You're a good cook?" Bliss opened the carton of milk Jesse handed her from the small refrigerator under her desk.

"My recipe file is slightly bigger than yours," Jessie teased. "I can reheat pizza."

The women finished their lunch then woke the children. The afternoon flew by as they played with the kids, having them expend their energy with the snowy day outside.

All the children had been picked up early since the snow had grown heavier. Darcy was the last one, and the sky was becoming darker.

"Lisa is late again," Jessie muttered under her breath so Darcy wouldn't hear.

"You go ahead. I'll stay with her and turn out all the lights and lock up."

"I can't ask you to do that. You've been opening every day."

"I don't mind. I can walk home. You live farther out of town. If you wait much longer, the roads will be too bad for you to get home." Bliss carefully went over all the nap mats with disinfectant, stacking them meticulously before putting them back in the closet.

"You don't have to twist my arm. I'm gone," Jessie said, going for her coat and purse.

Bliss went around the classroom, doing the chores to prepare for the next day and letting Darcy help. The girl looked adorable as she wiped down her desk as if it were the most important task in the world. When they finished, she read to Darcy until her foster mother came in to pick her up.

Lisa West looked around the empty room. "She's the last one?"

"Pick-up time is six." Bliss pointedly stared at the clock on the wall that showed seven-fifteen.

"My hair appointment ran late."

Bliss ignored the woman's lies, knowing full well no beauty salon in Treepoint stayed open past six.

She gently helped Darcy into her coat, buttoning it carefully. The coat wasn't very thick, unlike the one Mrs. West was wearing, nor had she brought a cap or gloves for the little girl.

"The temperature has dropped to almost zero. She doesn't have a hat—"

"I left the car running. She'll be fine." Lisa reached down, taking Darcy's hand before leading her outside into the blowing snow.

Bliss went to the window, watching Lisa uncaringly walk the child through the deep drifts. She only had on tennis shoes, which would be getting wet.

As the woman was about to get into the car, Bliss saw her stop to talk to someone walking down the sidewalk. It was Danny Owens, the town mayor. They stood, talking for several minutes in the freezing cold.

"Get in the car," Bliss spoke out loud in the empty room, looking over at the clock. They had already been standing there for over five minutes.

"Get in the car." Bliss was becoming more and more irritated. She could easily see Darcy shivering in the cold air under the street lamp. Still, the child never once moved to hurry Lisa up.

"Get in the fucking car!"

"Who are you talking to?"

Bliss spun around to see Drake standing in the room, looking at her strangely. She turned back to the window to see Lisa finally putting Darcy in the car.

"No one." Giving a sigh of relief, she moved to the desk to grab her purse and jacket. Then she grabbed the keys and went to the light switch to turn them out.

"Who were you watching out the window?"

Bliss knew Drake wouldn't stop until he had his answer. "I was watching Lisa keep Darcy out in the cold while she flirted with Danny."

"I thought you might have seen Stark."

"He's out of jail?" Bliss guessed trying to kidnap the town slut wouldn't constitute a high enough bond to delay him getting out.

"He posted bail an hour ago."

He probably had enough in that tacky wallet that was chained to his jeans to pay himself out.

"Merry freaking Christmas to me," Bliss snapped, going out the door. She waited just long enough for Drake to come outside before slamming it shut and locking it.

"It's going—"

"Please don't tell me it's going to be fine. I don't know why people say that. It's not. It never is." Bliss took off, walking angrily down the street.

"Wait! Where are you going?"

"To the house."

"I came to drive you. Get in my car."

Bliss wiped the snowflakes from her cheeks angrily. "I want to walk."

"If you need to blow off some steam, I'll drive us to the hotel and we can fuck until you feel better, but you're not going to walk in the freezing snow."

Bliss ignored him, taking a step away, only to find herself falling. She prepared to hit the icy pavement, but her momentum was stopped when Drake managed to catch her and lift her into his arms.

"What's wrong?" he demanded, knowing her well enough to see there was more bothering her than Stark.

"I hate Lisa. She couldn't care less about that little girl."

"Do you want me to find someone we can report her to?"

"No. Jessie told me today they have to find a new home for Darcy. Lisa has decided not to foster anymore. Jessie doesn't know how much longer she'll be at the daycare."

"I'm sorry. I know how attached you are to her."

Drake carried her to his car, and Bliss opened the door before Drake put her inside. He drove home carefully.

The snow on her driveway had already been cleared by the neighborhood boy she had hired. She hated shoveling snow, and it was one of the chores she had volunteered for since Ginny did most of the cooking. As long as the job was done, Bliss didn't think Ginny cared whether it was actually her out there shoveling or not.

Bliss got out of the car before Drake could carry her. "I can walk."

"You sure? I don't mind."

"I'm sure." Bliss's frustrated anger was beginning to dissipate.

Drake never let her moods affect his, and his calmness managed to make her feel as if she had more control over her own emotions.

"Want a cup of hot chocolate?" Bliss asked as she opened the front door.

"Will you put a shot of whiskey in it?"

"I'll see if I can find some." Bliss took off Ginny's coat, hanging it in the closet before going into the kitchen.

"Jessie says you're doing a great job."

She paused while pouring milk into the small pot as Drake took a seat at the table.

"When did you talk to Jessie?"

"Yesterday when she and her brothers came into the diner."

Bliss turned the stove on to heat the milk.

"Have you met her brothers yet?"

"No," Bliss answered absently. "Have you been out with Jessie?"

"No."

The shocked look on Drake's face relieved her. Jessie was a very attractive woman, and she was nice. Bliss had lost The Last Riders because of women just like her. The thought of losing Drake to another nice girl created a sick feeling in the pit of her stomach.

Bliss scooped in the powdered chocolate and stirred the creamy liquid quietly.

"Are you jealous?"

"Yes," Bliss admitted.

She felt his arms surround her, curling around her waist and pulling her backward against him. "You're the only woman I need, Bliss. I wanted you every time I saw you around town with The Last Riders. I would have joined if that was the only way to get you."

Bliss took the hot chocolate off the stove, pouring it into the mugs she had set out. "You wouldn't have made it past the initiation."

Bliss felt him stiffen behind her. "Why?"

"You have to fight the men to get in, and they're good."

"I'm beginning to feel insulted that you don't believe I can take care of myself or what's mine."

Bliss opened the cabinet, taking out the whiskey she had bought for him when he had asked if they had any the last time she made him hot chocolate. "You can't use guns. It's bare-handed fighting, and it's dirty. They don't play by any rules."

"I don't need my gun to win a fight. I've fought in—"

"These aren't high school fights," Bliss cut him off. "Some men haven't walked away when they're over. They want to make sure that, if you're a Last Rider, you can not only protect yourself but another member, as well. Besides, we're arguing over nothing. I'm not a Last Rider anymore."

"No, you're not." Drake released her, moving to the side to take his mug. "You miss it, don't you?"

"Not as much as I did. I miss the women who have been my friends for a long time. I miss Beth and Razer's twins. I miss the men." At that, Drake's face went hard and cold. "Not the sex. You're more than enough for me," she added hastily. "I miss Rider aggravating everyone, Lucky and Shade picking on each other, going to Viper when I need someone to talk to, Crash fixing my computer, and watching Cash fight and Razer with his kids. Mainly, I miss knowing no one would fuck with me because I belonged to them, that when I lay down at night to sleep, I wouldn't be woken up with a disgusting piece of filth between my legs. They never took without asking, and I always knew that what I gave, I wanted to give."

She lifted her mug, taking a sip of the warm hot chocolate. Damn, why did chocolate always make everything better?

"Sweet Bliss…I might not be able to give you everything they can, but I swear I can protect you. You only have to come to me when you need me. You went to them when you wanted something, now give me a chance to prove myself to you. I may surprise you. I even know a little bit about computers."

Bliss laughed. "I promise, the next time mine gives me trouble, you'll be the first one I call."

"You do that."

"You want marshmallows?"

"No, you're the only sweet I need with my chocolate."

"Aw, are you trying to be sweet to get in my pants?"

"Is it working?"

"Yes. Did I mention Ginny called me an hour ago? She's spending the night at Willa's house, so she won't have to drive to the clubhouse in the morning."

"You forgot to mention that."

"I am now," she teased.

"So, no hotel tonight? Damn, that's going to be nice. I had to give an extra fifty bucks last time we stayed for breaking the bed."

"I told you that ride was going to cost you." Bliss giggled.

The cell phone in her pocket chimed, indicating a text. Bliss reached into her pocket to take out the phone, going to her messages.

Devon's mom called. She found a couple of lice in his hair. He won't be back until we get a note from his pediatrician that he's clear. I'll check the rest of the children's hair when I get there in the morning. Night.

"Something up?"

"No, Jessie just needed to tell me something about work." She moved away from him to set her mug down on the counter. "I need a shower. I feel like I'm covered in glitter and glue. If you're hungry, you could order us a pizza. I won't be long."

ꕥ

Drake frowned at the kitchen door Bliss had rushed through. She had taken off like a scalded cat after her face had gone white when she had read the text message.

He would ask again what it was about when she came back. Whatever it was, it had bothered her. He almost texted Jessie, but he didn't want to deal with her crazy-assed brothers' questioning of why he had texted her.

They protected their sister like she was Fort Knox. Any man wanting to get close to her would have to take on those two knuckleheads, and Drake was man enough to admit he wasn't up for that job.

They lived deeper in the mountains than his cousins. Drake had never been on their property, because he was smart enough to obey the "No Trespassing" signs that were posted with several dire warnings.

The Porter land was next to Creech land. Behind both lay the Hayes land. The two sets of brothers were constantly bickering over the property line, and Greer and Holt were constantly trying to outdo each other with their signage. Personally, Drake thought Holt had won it with his large white sign with red paint spattered across a drawing of a stick figure with a target circling it.

Tate had asked him several times to find someone to survey the Porter land for him, but Drake had just snorted. No surveyor in the state of Kentucky would be willing to take on that job. It would be their last.

He ordered a couple of pizzas to be delivered, thankful Jace wasn't working with the weather getting so bad. The boys were both home, playing their computer games.

Drake finished his chocolate as he waited for Bliss, going into the living room where he turned on the television. However, when the thirty-minute comedy was almost over and the delivery driver had rung the doorbell, Bliss still wasn't downstairs.

He paid for the pizza then carried it to the kitchen before glancing at his watch, thinking Bliss should definitely have been downstairs by that point.

Abandoning the pizza, he went upstairs to her room, figuring he would find her blow-drying her hair in the bedroom. Instead, he heard the shower still on.

Coming to a stop, he listened and became fearful when he heard crying and Bliss's muffled voice coming from the bathroom. He hurriedly opened the bathroom door and was immediately hit with steam.

Once it cleared, Drake found Bliss crying in the shower stall.

"What the fuck!" He rushed forward, opening the shower door and staring down at her in dismay.

The water splashing on him was scalding hot, and Bliss's entire body was bright pink from the heat as she scrubbed her hair that was covered in a foul-smelling shampoo.

"Get them off! Get them off!" Her cries were gut-wrenching.

Drake reached in, adjusting the water temperature so it wasn't as hot. Hastily, he then jerked off his clothes before stepping into the shower with her.

"Get out! You'll catch them. I have to get them off," she moaned, still scrubbing her head through her cries.

Drake jerked her hands away from her scalp, ignoring her pleas as he swallowed back the bile rising in his throat at the damage she had done to herself.

He saw her nails were bloody and so was her scalp. Furthermore, tufts of hair were on the shower floor, slowly trailing a path to the drain.

"Stop it, Bliss." He grabbed both her hands again when they went right back to her head, forcing them behind her back until he could hold her still long enough to get the thick shampoo out of her hair. "What kind of shampoo is this?" he asked softly, her sobbing tearing at his heart.

"Lice shampoo."

Carefully tilting her head back, he rinsed her hair while she kept trying to get her hands free. The blood-tinged soap slid down her body, going down the drain.

"Quit struggling or you'll break both our necks."

She stopped fighting him immediately at the order, standing passively as he finished rinsing her off.

The medicated smell of the shampoo turned his stomach. Looking to the side of the shower, he saw a bottle with flowers on it. It nearly killed him to squeeze a small amount onto her ravaged head, but he did so and gently rubbed it in her hair with the palm of his hand then rinsed it off.

As soon as he was finished, he jerked her from the shower to dry her off. Seeing a blue robe on the back of the door, he put it on her himself before tying it closed. Then, picking her up, he carried her into the bedroom to sit her down on the side of the bed. Going back to the bathroom, he grabbed a fresh towel before returning to Bliss. Dazed, she hadn't moved from where he had left her.

"Why in the hell did you do that to yourself?" he asked as he gently dried what was left of her hair. When he pulled back the towel, spots of blood were on it.

"I can't get them again."

"What?"

"Lice." Her body shuddered. "They're terrible to get rid of."

"What makes you think you have lice?"

"Jessie told me Devon's mother found them on him. I'm around him all day."

"Did you check before you tore out most of your hair?"

"No, I didn't need to. I always catch them. When my mother and I lived on the streets, I kept them. I managed to get rid of them when she found a room for us to stay in for a while, but I caught them again when I lived with the Devil's Rejects. Evie helped me finally get rid of them when The Last Riders took me in."

"Jesus, is that why you keep your hair so short with all that gunk in it?"

"Yes. I don't want to catch them again." Bliss sobbed, her hands going to her head once more.

Drake jerked them back down. "Don't you fucking dare touch your hair again. There's barely any left."

"A single strand can have—"

"Bliss, believe me, nothing's alive on your head."

Drake made sure nothing was still bleeding before going to the bathroom to hunt for something to help her with the pain she was going to feel when the shock wore off.

Opening a drawer, he found the three joints he had given her. Taking one to the bedroom, he pulled a lighter out of his pocket.

"You need to take a couple of hits. It will help with the pain."

"It'll make me barf. I hate the taste of pot. It reminds me of the Devil's Rejects."

"Shit." Drake threw the pot into the trash can beside her bed. "Why didn't you tell me?"

"I didn't want you to stop doing it just because I didn't like it."

"Why the hell not?"

"I didn't want you to stop liking me." She stared up at him earnestly. Her hair was torn to fucking shreds, and she was worried over how he felt about her reaction to smoking pot? Shit.

He felt as if he had been kicked in his stomach.

"Jesus." Drake sat down on the bed next to her, putting his arm around her to pull her close. "I rarely smoke one unless I want to bash someone's face in. It mellows me out. I won't touch it again."

Bliss shook her head. "I don't mind. You'll resent me if you can't—"

"Shut up. Please, shut up. You're breaking my heart." The more time he spent with her, the more he noticed she always followed his lead, waiting to see how he would react to certain situations. If he showed the least bit of displeasure, she would always put what he wanted first. It drove him insane and he had hoped he had been wrong, that it was only the newness of them dating. It wasn't. It was a habit ingrained in her since she was fifteen.

She turned her face into his shoulder. "I'm sorry."

"Don't tell me you're sorry. You have nothing to be sorry for. You had a fucked-up childhood, you know that?"

"That's what Viper told me. He promised me The Last Riders wouldn't hurt me, that I could go anywhere I wanted and do anything I wanted. I begged him to join The Last Riders. It was the first home I ever had."

"They became your family." Drake had thought her connection with The Last Riders would eventually be severed as time went on, but he realized they would always remain in Bliss's heart. The Last Riders were a family not related by blood, but by the experiences and loyalty they shared.

"Yes. At least, they were until they started getting married, and they didn't need me anymore. If they didn't need me for sex, I was afraid they wouldn't want me anymore. I thought at least Shade would, because I tried to make him the happiest, but he only wanted Lily. Then Lucky fell for Willa, and he didn't need me, either. I kept trying to be what they needed me to be, but it was never enough. You'll eventually get tired of me, too."

"That's not going to happen."

"It will. It always does." Her voice was matter-of-fact. Bliss truly believed she wasn't worth holding on to.

"It's not going to happen. I'm telling you the truth, Bliss. I'm in love with you." He sighed. "I didn't have sex with you when we first started dating because I was courting you."

Her face peeked up from his shoulder. "You were?"

"I was until I realized it wasn't working. Then I went to plan B."

"Plan B?"

"To make you fall in love with my dick." He wanted to see the laughter back in her eyes.

"I have to admit it worked," she joked back, trying to mask the love shining in her eyes, too wary to tell him outright how she felt about him.

"It did?"

"Drake, that dick of yours is all any woman could ever want and more." Her shoulders shook with laughter. "I fell in love with you as soon as you pulled it out of your pants."

"That's not the first time I've heard that joke," he said wryly, and Bliss giggled harder.

Drake stared down at the beautiful sprite. She was less than half his size, but her spirit was the size of Mount Everest. She was filled with a capacity to love that was unequaled. She had stuck by a woman who had never been capable of giving her a stable home, but Bliss had given her mother one by giving her body to those who had taken and abused her.

Stark wasn't a young man. His long beard had been grizzled and grey. The thought of Bliss being subjected to that old bastard made Drake want to get his shotgun out. The only reason he hadn't gone after him yet was because he saw no reason to spend the rest of his life in prison when that jackass was going to make it easy for him.

Eventually, he would come back for Bliss, and when he did, Drake would kill him and shove Stark's own dick down his throat.

"What are we going to do about your poor hair?"

"It will grow back." Bliss self-consciously started to touch the short tufts, all that was left.

"Yes, it will. The next time you feel like you may have something in your hair, promise me you'll tell me, and I'll look and get them out without you hurting yourself." Drake reached out, pulling her hands down again.

"I couldn't let you do that."

"I got them out of Jace's hair twice when he was little. I'm an expert at them."

"Really?"

"Really." Drake curled his hand around her nape, lifting her head so his lips could tease hers. "I don't blame the little bastards. You're too sweet." He brought his mouth to her neck, teasing it as the robe fell off her shoulders.

"I thought you ordered pizza. What are you doing?"

"Making you fall in love with me all over again."

ꝏ ꝏ

Bliss hesitated with her hand on the door, trying to work up the courage to enter. Why in the hell was she here, anyway? She had lost her mind if she thought Sex Piston would help her.

Sighing, she dropped her hand away from the door and turned, bumping into someone about to enter the beauty salon.

"Excuse me—" Bliss's voice came to a stop when she recognized the woman glaring down at her.

"What are you doing here?" Killyama blocked her path to her car.

"I was going to get my hair done, but I can tell Sex Piston's busy, so I'll come back some other time." Bliss spoke in a rush.

Killyama's brows rose in surprise. "You came here to get your hair done?"

"Beth and Lily always said she's the best in the state." Bliss pulled Ginny's coat tighter against her, trying to keep the cold wind out.

"My bitch has to hear this." Killyama laughed, reaching out to open the door then herding her inside the shop.

Several women were sitting in chairs as they waited their turns. T.A., who was sitting behind the front desk, threw her a disgusted look, which Bliss was familiar with. It was the one most women gave her. Sex Piston and Crazy Bitch were both working on customers. The only one in Sex Piston's crew who was missing was Fat Louise, who must be at work at the nearby hospital.

"Why in the fuck is she here?" Sex Piston turned off the blow dryer. Her loud voice had the women in the shop waiting to witness the spectacle.

"That's what I asked her. She wants her hair done." Killyama threw her under the bus then took one of the empty beauty chairs to sit and watch.

"Why in the hell would I touch your hair?"

Bliss licked her lips nervously, tugging her red crocheted hat down farther over her head. "I don't know," Bliss mumbled before gaining some courage. "I was hoping you would put business over our personal issues. I can see I was wrong."

"Ya think? I wouldn't touch your skanky hair with a ten-foot pole. Get out," Sex Piston sneered.

Bliss nodded, turning to flee.

"Wait a minute. It true you're not with The Last Riders anymore?" Killyama's imperious voice cut through her fear.

Bliss hesitated. "Yes. I'm sure you think it's what I deserve."

"Yeah." Sex Piston went back to blowing out the hair of the brunette woman who was sitting in her chair.

Crazy Bitch took off the cape of the woman she was working on, telling her she was done. Bliss could tell the woman didn't want to miss the drama still going on inside the shop. She walked to the front desk, taking her time as she looked for her credit card.

Killyama leaned forward, placing her forearms on her thighs as she studied Bliss with narrowed eyes. "Take off your hat."

"There really isn't any need since Sex Piston doesn't want..." She tugged down her hat again, fidgeting with it fretfully.

Killyama stood, walking toward her with a determined stride. Bliss backed away, but she wasn't quick enough to dodge the hand that reached out to snatch the red hat away.

The blow-dryer went off again.

"What motherfucker did that to you?" Killyama snarled.

Bliss grabbed her hat back. "No one did this to me. I did it to myself."

"Why in the fuck would you do that?" Sex Piston put her blow-dryer down, coming toward her to gingerly touch the tufts of her remaining hair.

"I thought I might have lice."

Sex Piston didn't recoil in horror like Bliss expected. Instead, she gave her a stern look with her hands on her hips.

"You didn't check before you ripped out your hair?"

"No," Bliss chokingly admitted.

"Dammit! Christie, let Crazy Bitch finish you up." Sex Piston motioned for the woman to move to Crazy Bitch's chair before turning back to Bliss. "Take your coat off and sit your ass down," Sex Piston ordered, opening a drawer at her station and pulling out a pair of plastic gloves. She put them on matter-of-factly then began going through her hair. When she was finished, she took the gloves off and tossed them in the trash. "You don't have lice."

"Are you sure?" Bliss felt the heated fire of a blush stain her cheeks as everyone stared, waiting for the verdict.

"Yes. I'm sure. Bitch, I've seen my fair share of lice. Why didn't you ask someone to check before you ripped out your hair?"

"Because I felt them."

"You *felt* them?"

Bliss nodded helplessly. "When I was younger, I had lice several times. Some moms made their kids quit playing with me. I was finally able to get rid of them when I cut my hair off and Evie helped me."

Bliss wouldn't say that any of their expressions softened, but the hatred that was always so easily visible disappeared.

"You don't fuck Train anymore?" Killyama's sharp words startled Bliss at the sudden change in the conversation.

"What?" Bliss stared at her, dumbfounded.

"Do…you…fuck…Train…anymore?" Killyama spat out as if she was simpleminded.

"No. I. Don't," Bliss snapped, starting to get up, having had enough humiliation from these bitches. She wasn't going to take anymore.

Killyama leaned back in her chair. "Fix her hair," she ordered Sex Piston.

"What am I supposed to do with it? There's nothing left."

"You're bragging all the time about how good you are. Prove it. Fix her fucking hair."

"Since when do you care what her hair looks like?" Crazy Bitch twirled the poor woman around in her chair until Bliss thought she would get whiplash.

"Since she isn't fucking Train anymore."

"I don't know who would fuck her looking like this." Sex Piston reached into her drawer, pulling out a clipper. Draping a cape around her neck, she began shaving the rest of her hair off the sides.

Most women would have broken down in tears as their remaining hair fell to the floor. Bliss didn't. She simply watched in resignation as Sex Piston expertly glided the clippers around her head.

"Drake." Bliss found the name slipping from her lips.

"What?" T.A. asked from behind the counter, showing the other women hadn't lost interest. Gossip always ruled in a hair salon.

"Drake Hall doesn't have a problem fucking me with the way I look."

"He that good-looking realtor in Treepoint with his picture planted on those For Sale signs?" Sex Piston casually asked, setting down the clippers and picking up her scissors.

"Yes."

"He any good?" Killyama asked.

"Yes." Bliss straightened proudly in her chair, no longer hunching over. The women had gone from looking at her with pity to envy. That, she could deal with.

"Which is better, Train or Drake?" Killyama's booted foot began tapping on the floor.

Bliss was afraid to answer the strange woman's question.

"Well?" Impatience laced her voice.

"It's impossible to answer that question. It's like comparing apples and oranges." Bliss hoped her answer would let her off the hook. It didn't.

"No, it isn't. If you could only have one of them in bed, who would it be?"

"Both," Crazy Bitch joked.

"Shut the fuck up," Killyama growled at her and then turned to Bliss. "Answer the damn question."

"Drake."

Killyama's face relaxed into a serene mask. "I'll make sure to pass that information along to Train the next time I see him." She looked like she was already enjoying the thought of telling Train that Drake was better.

"You don't like Train?" Bliss tried not to wince when Sex Piston combed out her hair.

"She loves him," Crazy Bitch said in a sing-song voice.

"Bitch, don't make me get up," Killyama threatened her friend. "I don't love that fucker. I can't stand him."

"That's for sure. You prefer him lying down on his back," Sex Piston joked, standing back to admire her handiwork. "There. That's the best I can do."

Bliss felt her head. The sides were all buzzed off, leaving a small tuft of hair across the top of her scalp in a lopsided Mohawk. Sex Piston had sprayed mousse until it was spiked up. It wasn't perfect, but it was much better than it had been.

"You look cool," T.A. complimented, coming closer to look. "You did a good job, Sex Piston."

"I know," she said, taking off the cape.

Bliss stood, following T.A. back to the counter to pay. T.A rang her up while she put her coat back on. Bliss then paid, leaving a generous tip, before she went back to Sex Piston's station.

"Thank you. I appreciate you fixing the mess I made."

Sex Piston gave her a hard look. "I don't like bitches who try to take other women's men. We aren't ever going to be best friends, but you can come back until I get your hair straightened out."

Bliss nodded, putting her red hat in her pocket.

She stared at Killyama. "Train likes it when you rub his shoulders. It makes him horny."

The women around her tensed, waiting for Killyama to beat the shit out of her.

"Anything else?" Interest sparked in her eyes.

"He's a whore for blow jobs." Bliss racked her brains for anything else that could help the woman. "Oh, yeah, he *really* likes blow jobs."

Killyama stood, and Bliss tensed, waiting for her reaction.

"Sit down, bitch. Tell me what else Train likes."

Her peace offering had been accepted.

Chapter Fourteen

"Where's Darcy today? She never misses," Bliss asked Jessie as soon as breakfast was finished.

"She won't be coming anymore. She was placed in another foster home. The family she will be staying with has six kids, and the mother stays home with them."

"Six kids? Darcy will be the seventh?"

"Yes." Jessie left to wipe up the spilled orange juice on the counter, and Bliss took a group of three children to read them a story.

"Are you okay, Miss Bliss?"

"I'm fine, Marcus." Bliss furiously blinked back the tears threatening to fall.

"Why are you crying, then?"

"I have something in my eye."

Bliss managed to hold back more tears as she finished the story.

"Who wants to make a list for Santa?" she asked when she was done. "We'll put them on the wall so your parents will see and tell Santa when he calls."

"Santa doesn't call!" Anna called out. "We go to the supermarket and tell him."

"I saw him at the bank." Marcus pushed Anna back so he could be heard.

"Santa is a busy man. We'll make the list in case you forgot to tell him something."

"Yay! I forgot to tell him I wanted a new car so Mama will quit crying about ours in the morning when it doesn't start," Marcus said, grabbing a piece of construction paper.

Bliss sat down at the large table where the children were working.

Anna raised her head to stare at her quizzically. "What do you want for Christmas, Miss Bliss?"

"I already have everything I want."

"I wanted a new bike last year, and Santa didn't bring it." Cory glued a picture of a bright red bike onto his paper.

Jessie and Bliss had spent lunch cutting out over a hundred things the children could want for Christmas. Since they were sure the parents wanted the tradition of helping their children make their Christmas lists, they had come up with letting them glue the pictures as an alternative.

"You must have been bad. That's why you didn't get it," Anna explained without sympathy. "I got the doll I wanted."

"Did you get everything you wanted when you were little, Miss Bliss?"

Bliss was only half paying attention to them, her mind on Darcy. She took one of the papers, grabbing a few pictures to fiddle with. "When I was little, I wanted a coat. It had a furry hood and was cream-colored. I thought it was the prettiest thing I had ever seen. It was in a department store my mother and I passed every day." Bliss didn't tell them they would walk past the store on the way to the free lunch the church fed the homeless.

"Did you get it for Christmas?"

"No, I didn't." It was the last time she had truly believed in Santa Claus and that her life would be better than it was. She had only been five years old.

"Were you bad?" Anna whispered.

"I must have been."

"Can I glue your pictures down?"

"What?"

"Can I glue your pictures down?" Marcus repeated. "I'm finished with mine."

"Go ahead." Bliss slid the paper over she had been absently playing with. "When you're done, let's wash our hands and do circle time."

The children talked about their Christmas plans as they finished. Their excitement was increasing each day as it grew closer.

She had already picked out presents for Drake, Jace and Cal. Drake wasn't going to be happy about them, but he would get over it when she gave him a blow job. The man was putty in her hands as soon as her mouth went anywhere near his dick.

Bliss was putting the books back in the reading center after closing time when Lisa West came in, despite the closed sign outside. Jessie had been about to turn the lights out; she was just waiting for Bliss to finish straightening up for the following day.

"What can I help you with, Lisa?"

"I just wanted to drop off the check for Darcy's last week." She took it out, handing it to Jessie.

Bliss put on Ginny's coat as she eavesdropped.

"I was sorry to lose Darcy. We'll all miss her."

"I will, too." The fakeness in Lisa's voice made Bliss want to rip out her heavily styled curls.

"Maybe her new foster mother will bring her in for the Christmas party we're hav—"

"I wouldn't count on it. The State already took her away from her new foster home after only a few hours. She's in the hospital in Jamestown. The worker told me when I took the last of her things by the office."

"She's in the hospital?" Bliss broke into the conversation.

"Yes, they took her there this morning. The worker seemed to think it's the flu." Lisa arched a sculpted eyebrow, letting her know she didn't think it was appropriate for her to butt in to the conversation. Bliss could give a flying fuck what that high-class bitch thought of her.

Not caring that the two women were staring after her, she left abruptly without another word. In a nanosecond, she was behind the wheel of her car and driving as fast as she could toward the county road that led to Jamestown.

The thought of the little girl alone in the hospital with only strangers made her want to go back and beat the crap out of the woman who hadn't cared enough to even call to check on her condition.

Her mind played back over the image of Darcy standing outside with Lisa in the cold. She should have gone outside and put her in the car herself.

"Please, be okay…Please, be okay." Bliss was afraid, like all her wishes, it wouldn't come true.

ꕤ

Drake was about to turn his computer off then meet Bliss at the diner when his cell phone rang.

"If you're calling me again about freezing your balls off, I'm leaving now. You can go home in a—"

"Your woman just took off in her car." Greer's casual statement sent his heart pounding.

"Where was she going?" Bliss was supposed to walk over to his office after the daycare closed.

"How in the hell do I know? She was in her car and driving away before I could get out of this tree. My ass is numb."

"I told you to watch her from your truck," Drake snapped. When he had asked his cousins to take turns watching over Bliss when he couldn't, they had all agreed for a price. Greer, of course, hadn't wanted to do it without an expensive incentive, saying it would be boring. Drake had made it worth his while.

"That wouldn't have been any fun."

Drake ground his teeth together. "Where…is…she?"

"I…do…not…know."

So help him God, he was going to strangle his cousin.

Drake shut his laptop, getting to his feet. "Which direction did she go?"

"Out of town."

"Which direction?" Drake was almost at his car.

"Toward Jamestown."

Drake started his car. "I'll try to catch up."

"Why are you going to do that?"

Drake strangled the steering wheel. "Because I want to know where she's going, asshole."

"There's no need to get nasty. Dustin will call when she gets where she's going."

"Dustin's following her?"

"Yes."

"You could have told me that to begin with!"

"That wouldn't have been any fun."

"You know that new truck I promised you if you and your brothers kept an eye on her?"

"Yeah?" Greer's voice became wary.

"It just got downgraded from a half-ton to a basic pickup. Fuck with me again, and you'll be driving that old truck of yours until it's so rusted you'll be able to see through it."

Chapter Fifteen

Bliss jumped up when she saw Drake walking toward her in the waiting room. His face was pale and worried. She didn't know how he had known where she was, and she didn't care right then.

"Why are you here?" he asked. "Are you sick? What's wrong?"

She grabbed his arm, frantically shoving him toward the woman behind the registration desk. "She won't let me see Darcy. Make her let me see her."

"You're okay? It's Darcy who's sick?"

Bliss nodded frantically. "Make her let me see her. Please, Drake. I'll make it up to you later. I promise..."

Drake came to a sudden stop. "Go sit down and let me talk to her."

Bliss looked like she was about to argue, but she saw from his expression that it wouldn't help. Blinking back her tears, she went to sit down, but he stopped her.

"Don't ever think you have to bribe me like that ever again. If you want something from me, all you have to do is fucking ask. Got it?"

"Yes."

Drake's expression softened. "Now, go sit down and let me get you in to see her. Okay?"

"Okay."

His confidence soothed her as no other reassurances could. She took a seat and watched as Drake talked to the woman. From her expression, Bliss could tell she wasn't telling him shit.

Her hands gripped each other tightly to keep herself from going back to his side. Her resolve almost broke when he stepped away from the desk to take out his cell phone. He talked for several minutes before he handed his phone to the woman behind the desk.

Her attitude underwent a drastic change after whoever was on the other line spoke to her. She then handed the phone back to Drake, who returned it to his pocket.

He continued to stand there, talking to her for several seconds, before he walked away and came back to Bliss.

"Let's go. She's not here. They've airlifted her to the children's hospital in Lexington."

Bliss's knees buckled but Drake caught her, steadying her.

"Why? What's wrong with her?"

"Pneumonia."

ꕥ

The drive to Lexington was three hours long. Bliss felt as if the trip were never-ending.

"You hungry?"

She felt too sick to her stomach to even think of food. "No. How did you get them to tell you?"

"I called her social worker, and because I have guardianship over Cal, they let me have the information."

"Oh, God. Cal is going to be worried sick. Should we call?" Bliss reprimanded herself for not thinking of calling Cal. He deserved to know what was going on with his sister more than she did.

"I texted Rachel. She and Cash are driving him down. They're not far behind us."

"Her father?"

"I'll call the prison that son of a bitch is in when we find out how she is."

"She has to be bad to be airlifted out, doesn't she?"

"Yes."

A small sob escaped Bliss at his answer. "She was looking forward to Christmas."

"She's going to be all right, Bliss."

Drake couldn't understand, but she did. Sometimes, there just weren't the happy endings you read about in books.

"How much longer?"

"Another thirty minutes."

Bliss prayed for the little girl the whole way. It was only when they were entering the lobby that she thought to ask if they would be allowed to see her.

"I'll get us in."

Drake was as good as his word, although it took a frustrating hour before they were led to her room. Darcy was lying in a bed while a woman she didn't recognize sat in a chair, watching the television on the wall.

She stood up when Bliss went to Darcy's bedside.

"Who are you?"

"We're family," Drake answered. "You can call your supervisor. Sit outside. If we need you, we'll let you know."

"I can't leave her side," the woman argued.

"Call your supervisor."

Bliss didn't care if the woman stayed or left as long as they let her see Darcy.

The little girl was hooked up to an IV pump. Her face was flushed, and her cheeks were tear-streaked.

"Darcy?" Bliss whispered. She didn't want to wake her, but she wanted the girl to know she wasn't alone anymore.

"Miss Bliss?" Darcy's eyes fluttered open.

"Hi, sweetie. I heard you were sick, so I want to stay with you until you feel better. Is that okay?"

She nodded. "I'm afraid. The needles hurt."

Bliss had to bend lower to hear her whispered words.

"They're giving you medicine to make you feel better." God, how she was praying the life-saving drugs were working.

Her hand with the IV lifted to touch the side of Bliss's head. "Are you sick?"

"No. I just got a haircut."

"I don't like it."

"It'll grow back."

"It has to grow back a lot." Darcy's eyes were transfixed on the missing hair.

Bliss touched the little girl's soft cheek. "I know."

"Do you think Santa can find me here?"

"Yes."

"Are you sure?"

Bliss hid her anguish, remembering clearly what Darcy had told her what she wanted for Christmas. The girl was doomed for disappointment wherever she was going to be Christmas morning.

"I'm sure," Bliss stated positively. "Santa wouldn't miss stopping for you. You've been the best little girl in the world." Even if Darcy couldn't have her mother back for Christmas, Bliss promised herself she would shower the little girl with the other things she had glued down on her paper. She had already purchased the majority of them.

"Really?"

"Really. I should know, you made my Christmas wish come true."

"How?"

Bliss wiped the tearstains away from Darcy's flushed cheeks. "You smiled at me when you opened your eyes. Your smile is the only Christmas present I need."

"Can you stay with me?"

"I'm not going anywhere," Bliss promised.

"I can't find my blanket."

Bliss turned to find Drake, already knowing it was another problem he could fix.

"I'm on it." Drake reached out, squeezing Darcy's toes through the blanket. "Cal's here to see you."

"Bubby's here?" Hope filled the little girl's voice.

Bliss was going to get Drake to talk to Darcy's social worker about increasing how much time Cal could spend with his sister each week.

"I'll get him and bring him here."

"Okay. Don't forget my blanket."

"I won't."

Darcy looked up at her after Drake left. "I like him."

"I do, too."

Darcy dozed off not long after she saw Cal, and Bliss sat by her bedside for the rest of the night, refusing to leave even when Drake told her that he and Cal would stay. He didn't argue, having a nurse bring in a small cot for her to sleep on.

"You go to a hotel with Cal," she told him. "I'll be all right here with her."

"Jace is outside. They can get a room and come back in the morning."

"You're staying?"

"Bliss, I keep on telling you I'm not going anywhere without you."

The conviction in his voice tempted her to believe in him. Just once, she really wished she believed in miracles.

Chapter Sixteen

"Are you sure she'll be all right?" Bliss could see her breath in the cold air as they stood in the patient loading area in front of the hospital.

Darcy was going home after a week in the hospital. The little girl had been happy to hear she was leaving until Bliss had explained it would be after Christmas before she would be able to see her again.

"For the thousandth and one time, yes, I'm sure. She has to go back to the new foster home the State placed her in. We can't stop it."

"I know."

It didn't make it any easier as Bliss waved good-bye to Darcy, who was waving at her from the car window.

"It won't be for long," Cal vowed, also waving at his sister. "As soon as I get back to town, I'm going to try to get guardianship of her. The semester is over, so not only am I done with school but I'm eighteen now."

"What about going into the service?" Drake's surprise showed it was the first time Cal had mentioned the plan.

"Darcy is my sister. Family comes first."

"You've been dreaming of going into the service for the last two years," Drake replied.

"You don't always get what you want. I was being selfish by thinking I could leave her behind. I was hoping she would be happier with the Wests, since they have more than I could ever offer her. Now she's at a different home, and I'm not going to sit back and watch her being moved from home to home. It's not going to happen. I won't take the chance on anything else happening to her."

"Have you told Jace?" Drake asked.

"I'll tell him on the way back to Treepoint. He'll understand."

"Yes, he will." Drake patted him on his shoulder. "I'll see you back in town." He left to get the car as Jace pulled up to pick up Cal.

He stepped forward to get in, but Bliss stopped him.

"Cal…I wish there was something I could do. I would take her, but the courts would laugh in my face if I applied to be a foster parent."

He looked at her in shock. "You want Darcy?"

"More than anything in the world. I love her, but the State will want character references, and I can't give many that would convince them to trust me with her."

Cal leaned down, placing a kiss on her cheek before getting into the car. "I can think of several people who would give you a great character reference, but I won't let her go to another foster home. The next home she goes to is going to be her forever home."

"That takes me out." Bliss hid her disappointment. "I haven't even found my own."

The house she lived in was just that: a house. Ginny had given Willa a down payment, so it was Ginny's forever home, not hers.

Drake pulled up behind Jace's car as Cal rolled down his window.

Bliss leaned down into it. "You two be careful driving back. It's a long drive for your junker."

"Don't insult the car. It's better than walking," Jace jokingly boasted.

"Not much," Bliss teased, stepping back.

"It's beautiful." Cal smiled, rolling the window up in starts and stops.

"We need to fix that," she heard Jace tell Cal as they pulled away.

She got into Drake's car, mumbling.

"What did you say?"

"That car is ugly as shit."

"It's a classic."

"Who did you buy it from?"

"Crazy Bitch."

"Doesn't that say it all?"

ꕥ ꕥ

Bliss tiredly turned out the daycare lights. The Christmas party had wiped her out. Anyone who didn't believe candy affected children needed to work in a daycare during a party. They had practically been hanging from the lights when the parents had started arriving. She had already told Jessie that the following year, they were having vegetable trays, and that was all.

"Are you still going to be around next year?"

Bliss realized then what she had unconsciously said.

"I guess so, unless another parent packs in a tray of Willa's cupcakes. Then I want that day off or double pay."

"I'm not making any promises. Those cupcakes are worth hiring extra help for the day."

On that note, Bliss offered to close up for her.

"I appreciate it. I'm meeting my brothers at the diner for dinner."

"Have a Merry Christmas. I'll see you next week."

Jessie left, still laughing about the kids' sugar high.

It was the day before Christmas Eve, and the daycare wouldn't reopen until the second day of January. Bliss was going to miss the children, but she would definitely enjoy the break.

The cold wind hit her as soon as she opened the door. She hurriedly closed and locked it, dreading getting into her cold car. When was she going to remember to automatically start the car so it would be warm when she got inside?

It was in the empty side parking lot where Drake was usually parked because he had been following her home after work. However, he had called earlier to tell her he was showing Cal an apartment and would see her later that night.

She was almost to her car when she heard motorcycles coming down the street. Wondering which Last Riders were riding, she stopped to look. That was her first mistake. Her second was not running like hell when Stark rode in, accelerating his motorcycle toward her.

She simply froze, putting her hands up to cover her eyes, temporarily blinded by his headlight and the dozen others following behind him.

"You have a choice, bitch. Either get on, or the only thing going in that pussy of yours from now on will be the worms eating your dead body."

Bliss lowered her hands to see he had a gun pointed toward her face.

"You might as well shoot. I'd rather be dead than have you touch me!" Bliss yelled, making no effort to run. She wasn't going to try to outrun a bullet.

When Stark grabbed the scarf around her neck that was blowing in the wind, Bliss tried to yank it back. She gave a strangled scream of terror when she saw his hand disappear in a red mist of blood. It splattered both her and Stark, and she fell backward as gunfire erupted around her.

She landed on her ass as the bikers surrounding her fell off their motorcycles, one after the other.

"Get in your car!" Dustin Porter yelled, running across the parking lot toward her.

Bliss got on her knees, crawling toward her car and whimpering, expecting to feel a bullet any second.

She reached her car just as a huge biker dropped next to her, his face no longer there.

"Oh, God…Oh, God," Bliss chanted in terror.

"Move that ass!" Greer Porter yelled, stepping in front of her, his rifle blasting a biker who had been about to shoot.

"I'm trying!" Bliss screamed back at the man who had already picked another target, shooting a large biker who was trying to escape.

Greer laughed. "Like shooting sitting ducks."

"Oh, my God, you're crazy!" Bliss rose up on her knees to reach her car door handle.

She froze again, watching as Tate Porter drove his pickup into the parking lot, ramming the bikers with his truck. Bliss wanted to vomit. He was running them down without mercy.

She finally had her car door open and was trying to scramble inside when she felt herself picked up and tossed in. She heard the door slam as she landed, sprawled across the front bucket seats.

"Stay down!" Drake's harsh voice startled her into rising, her own safety forgotten as she struggled to see what was going on outside.

"Drake!" Bliss screamed as he ran toward Stark, who was shooting at him.

She saw blood blossom on his shirtsleeve before he threw himself at Stark, knocking both of them to the ground. Drake's fists pounded Stark's face before he reached into his back pocket and pulled out a knife.

Bliss watched in dismayed horror as Drake buried his knife in the biker's throat then raised it again to bury it in his chest, dragging it downward in one stroke.

What he did next had her turning away, unable to watch any longer. The devil wasn't going to be left with a choice that time. Stark was on his way to hell.

Chapter Seventeen

"I ain't taking credit for that."

Drake stood, wiping his bloody knife off on his pants leg. "Don't worry, Greer. I'll make sure Knox knows I did it."

"Is he dead?" he asked, bringing his rifle down to poke at the limp body.

Tate rolled his eyes at Greer.

"What in the hell do you think?" Dustin said, looking between the brothers blocking his view. "He's sucking his own dick."

"Drop your guns," Tate ordered. "Here comes Knox. I don't want to give him any excuse to shoot us."

The four men dropped their weapons to the pavement as the sheriff parked his squad car in the middle of the street. There were too many dead bodies and broken bikes for him to pull into the parking lot.

"You think he's going to be pissed?" Greer asked.

"Look at that face. What do you think?" Drake prepared for the blasting Knox was going to give for not calling him and letting the police handle Stark.

"Any of them alive?" Knox asked, his face a calm mask as he walked up, looking over the bodies littering the ground.

"I just shoot them if they move. None's moved, so I'd say they're all pretty much dead," Tate answered, keeping his eyes on the bodies as if one would suddenly jump up.

Drake really wondered sometimes if his mother had been adopted into the Porter family.

Knox winced when he saw Stark's body. "Who's responsible for that?"

Drake opened his mouth to confess, but was beaten to the punch.

"I did it," Greer lied.

"I guess I need to call the coroner. I better count how many body bags he'll need." Knox pulled his radio out, walking around the parking lot and poking the bodies with the toe of his boots as he talked to dispatch.

"Want to tell me why you changed your mind?" Drake asked Greer. "I did it, and I'm going to tell him that when he comes back."

"Want to spend Christmas Eve with your woman or with paperwork for Knox?" Greer patted him on the back "Merry fucking Christmas. And my new truck better be sitting outside the sheriff's office when I get done."

Drake couldn't help laughing at his cousin. Greer would have the biggest truck he could buy.

He had called Drake when he had seen the large group coming into town. They had been waiting for the bikers to attack. Drake had actually believed they would try to get her when she was farther away from the sheriff's office, though, so he had been waiting down the street at the cut-off to her house.

When he heard the shooting, he had come running in time to kill the one his cousins had promised to save for him.

All of a sudden, he had the air knocked out of him when Bliss threw herself into his arms.

"Are you okay? I called an ambulance for you."

"Why?" He gave her a bewildered look.

"You've been shot." Bliss tried to pull back to look at his arm, but Drake pulled her back into his arms.

"I'm fine. It passed through."

Knox came back then with the yellow tape to mark off the parking lot. "Do you Porters ever leave anyone alive to tell their side of the story?"

"Technically, he ain't a Porter. His ma is my dad's sister," Greer corrected.

"I have as much Porter blood as you," Drake repeated the same phrase he had said numerous times over the years, proudly proclaiming what he had been thinking about denying just minutes before.

Greer looked down at Stark's dead body. "I'm going to agree with you this time."

Drake held Bliss tighter, the way she liked to be held when she was afraid.

Out of the corner of his eye, he saw a shadow move from behind the building then another following, heading toward the church across the street. Three more joined them from different vantage points. Drake didn't have to see their faces to recognize them.

The Last Riders hadn't left Bliss unprotected; they had been watching over her, too.

Stark hadn't stood a chance. He had ridden into his own execution.

ஐ ௸

It was after midnight when they returned to his home. Bliss had won, making him go to the hospital to be stitched up.

Jace and Cal were spending the night with Jace's mother and would be back Christmas morning.

"Guess who's spending the night?" Drake taunted as she trailed behind him to his bedroom.

"They aren't home?"

"Not until Christmas Day."

"We can spend two nights together?"

"Yes.

"This Christmas is turning out to be the best one I've ever had!"

"Wait until I give you my present. It will put it over the top."

Bliss sat down on the end of the bed, using her feet to make herself bounce on the mattress. "What did you get me?"

"You have to wait until Christmas morning," Drake told her as he pulled off his bloody clothes.

"Is it bigger than the palm of my hand?"

"A little bigger."

"Is it this size?" Bliss moved her hands several inches apart, mimicking the size of his dick.

"A little bigger."

"Wow. Now I'm really curious." She stopped bouncing. "Men's dicks don't get bigger as they get older, do they?"

"No, they typically shrink."

"Is that true?" She had an adorably bewildered look on her face. "How did I not know this?"

"Because men don't want women to know."

Damn, I bet they don't. He doesn't have an inch I want to give up.

"I'm only asking out of curiosity, but how much do they shrink? A little or a lot?"

"Not much. Only a little…about half an inch."

"That's all? That's okay, then. I mean, that's good for you. You don't have to worry like some men would." Bliss started bouncing on the bed again.

"Bliss, I don't think you're going to have to worry about how much my dick is going to shrink."

"Why not?"

"Because all I need to satisfy you is my tongue." Drake threw his dirty shirt at her as he went into the bathroom.

"Ew. Stark's blood is all over that."

"That's why I gave it to you. Figured you deserved it for everything that bastard put you through."

"I should frame it, but I won't. I'll burn it like he is right now. By the way, this shirt isn't my Christmas present, is it?"

She smiled when she heard his laughter over the shower.

"Make sure you don't get those stitches wet," she called out.

"Why don't you come in here and keep them dry for me?"

Not needing any more of an invitation, Bliss wiggled her ass out of her jeans then took off her blouse.

She was about to grab a condom from his nightstand where he always kept them but stopped. They had never fucked without protection, even though there was no chance of her getting pregnant.

She closed the drawer, empty-handed.

Drake was soaping his body when she opened the shower door.

"Let me." Bliss took the washcloth he was using, rubbing it across his chest at the same time her hand went to his already hard cock. "I see you've been warming yourself up." She ran her hand over the sensitive slit, not lingering before she stroked downward to cup his balls.

He brought his hand between her thighs, sinking a large finger deep inside of her. "This is all I need to warm me up." His finger moved deeper. "Want to give me a hint about *my* present? Is it bigger than the palm of my hand?"

"Yes," Bliss moaned, going back to stroking his cock.

"Is it bigger than my dick?"

"Yes," Bliss moaned. "It's not fair to ask me questions when you're finger-fucking me."

"Being fair is for sissies."

"You're definitely not a sissy." *Thank God for that*, she thought when he inserted another finger, steadily fucking her.

Bliss wrapped a thigh around his hip, pressing the heel of her foot against his firm ass. Then she licked at his pebbled nipple, raking her teeth against the tip.

Drake moved her thigh down so she was standing on her feet again. "It's too slippery to fuck you like this. I don't want to be the next episode on *Sex Sent Me to the ER*."

"Drake, if fucking you was going to send me to the ER, it would have happened the first time. Baby, you're big, but you aren't that big," she taunted.

"Is that so? Let's see how big it feels when I put it where I want to." Drake ran a soapy finger between her ass cheeks.

Bliss lost her smile. "Hell no! I'm not that crazy!" She tried to move past him to the door; instead, she found herself bent over the marble seat at the end of the shower. "Drake!"

"Hush!" Drake smacked her ass then ran his hand up her back, leaning over her so she couldn't rise. "If you don't like it past the first inch, I'll stop."

"The head will kill me before you get an inch inside of me."

Out of the corner of her eye, she saw him take a tube of lube from the shelf.

"You keep lube in the shower?"

"I believe in planning ahead," Drake mocked as he smeared a heavy amount of lube along the length of his dick. "It might be easier if you don't watch."

"You're an ass," she snapped, becoming aroused despite her misgivings.

Bliss felt the spongy tip of his cock press against the rosebud of her ass.

"Oh, God."

"You have a habit of doing that. I really wish you would find something else to say right now. It kind of kills the mood."

"Good." Bliss tried to rise again, but Drake pressed her back down.

"It doesn't kill it that much."

Bliss began to feel the pressure of him trying to enter her tight hole. "It's not going to fit."

"It'll fit."

The pressure began to turn into pain.

"Relax, Bliss." Drake slid his hand to her pussy, rubbing her clit then sinking his finger back inside of her, finger-fucking her as he managed to guide his cock inside her tight hole.

"You better make this good, or we're never doing this again," she warned.

"You'll like it. I know I am." Drake hissed between clenched teeth.

Bliss tried to focus on the pleasure going on inside her pussy, ignoring the burning pain Drake's cock was making as he entered her. She felt each centimeter of his cock, the ridges and veins as he pushed farther inside.

"I better wake up to a cherry-red Porsche sitting in my driveway Christmas morning."

"I want you to enjoy this. I'll stop." She felt Drake begin to pull back.

"Don't you dare! I want to, I just talk too much when I'm nervous."

"Then let's stop. We can do this another night."

Bliss went tense, not paying attention to anything except the words that had just come out of his mouth.

"If I never wanted to do this, would you mind?"

"No. If I do anything you don't want to do, tell me. There are hundreds of ways to have sex. If one doesn't work for you, we do something else." He slapped her ass again, exclaiming, "Jesus, Bliss! Haven't you figured out that your happiness is what makes me happy, too?"

Bliss felt every bone in her body melt at his words.

She put her hand on his hip to tug him closer. "It takes a lot to make me happy, but you do have what it takes to get the job done."

"You sure?"

Bliss lifted her ass higher. "Yes. Just go slow."

"Why? If it hurts that bad—"

"It feels so good I'm afraid I won't last long."

"I'm about to come, and I'm barely inside you." He paused before saying, "What if I said I would buy you a diamond ring if you don't come for five minutes?"

"Really?" Bliss attempted to wrap her swirling thoughts around what he was trying to tell her.

"Yes, but you have to quit talking. I can't concentrate when you do."

Bliss held her breath as he began pumping inside of her. His thrusts set off every sensitive muscle, and her nerve endings began to explode.

"Slower."

He rubbed her clit with his thumb. Damn, he was dexterous. It would take two of The Last Riders to heat her up to the extent that had her body begging for a climax.

"How long has it been?" she asked.

"Only a minute."

She wasn't going to make it. She wanted that ring, but she really, really wanted to come right then. She didn't know how much longer she was going to be able to hold it back.

Bliss couldn't keep her ass still. She began fucking back against him, almost climaxing when he glided his fingers deeper inside of her and his cock went higher.

She bit her lip to keep from coming. She needed motivation to deny herself an orgasm that promised to be memory-worthy.

"Can I ask one question?"

Drake's sweat- and water-drenched forehead dropped to her back. "For fuck's sake, go ahead." He was easily in the same predicament she was.

"Are we talking a regular diamond ring or an engagement ring?"

"An engagement ring. Now, will you please shut up?"

"Yes, right after you tell me how many carats."

"Right now, I'm thinking it's going to be pretty damn small."

Bliss figured she still had time to change his mind on that.

Spreading her legs wider, she lowered until her tits were pressed against the marble seat. She allowed her body to relax when his hips moved forward, rocking into her. The sensual movements drew a hiss from him and increased her own pleasure.

Damn, this was more than memory-worthy. This was worthy of writing it down in a diary so that, when she was a hundred years old, she could look back and know nothing had ever beaten this one blow-your-freaking-mind, hope-you-don't-break-your-neck shower fuck.

She breathed a sigh of relief when she felt his balls against her ass. He wasn't going to last much longer, either.

"How long?" Bliss begged.

"Four and a half minutes."

She went up on the tips of her toes as he continued to thrust in and out of her.

"One, don't make me come. Two, don't make me come. Three, don't make me come."

"What are you doing now?"

"Counting off seconds."

She moaned as he fucked her into an orgasm that had her losing count. Every time she thought she was finished coming, his cock set off another series of explosions.

As her knees went weak, Drake had to hold her steady as he turned her until he was sitting on the seat. Then she was the one setting the pace, making sure her ass cheeks rubbed against his stomach each time she brought her weight down.

Drake caught a breast in each of his hands as his mouth went to her shoulder, biting down softly.

She couldn't hold back her scream when she felt his cock begin to jerk in her ass, and she fell back against his chest, panting as she came hard enough for her mind to go dark.

"Bliss, are you all right? Bliss?"

"Did I make it five minutes?"

"You actually lasted eight. I was enjoying myself."

"That wasn't fair." Her head fell back on his shoulder.

"I'll make it up to you. I'll buy you a bigger ring."

She slid her hand down his thigh. She loved touching him.

His hand curled around her stomach, easing the muscles still quivering. He liked to pet her as much as she did him.

Sex with the Devil's Rejects had never been given freely. Sex with The Last Riders had been to tie them to her. Sex with Drake was what it was supposed to be—two people learning to make the other happy and feel good, bonding together to make it something more than sex. That was why the name for it was different. It was called making love.

That was also why, no matter what dangerous situations she had been in during her lifetime, she was never more afraid than she was right then. If she lost Drake like she had lost The Last Riders, she would never recover. That was the way the men felt about their wives, what she had tried to come between.

"What's wrong?" Drake broke through her thoughts.

"I'm a terrible person."

"You're a wonderful person."

"No, I'm not. If a woman tried to break us up, I would scratch her eyes out. I tried to cause trouble with the wives of the club, and I wouldn't have cared if I had broken them up." Bliss covered her face with her hands, too ashamed to let Drake look at her.

"You were trying to hold on to the safety in your life the only way you knew how. You didn't trust them to want to protect you because they cared about you. You didn't trust in the club itself. You gave them your loyalty, but you held back your trust, just like with me. You can give me your body a million times, but if you don't give me your trust, you're not giving me you. I can wait for you to learn that I can keep you safe."

"You more than proved that with Stark. The Last Riders couldn't have done better."

"I'll take that as a compliment."

"Why aren't you jealous of them?" she asked, knowing most men would resent her past with the bikers.

The Last Riders were always around town. Viper was involved in almost as many organizations as Drake. She had even confessed the meaning of the tattoo on her breast on a snowy afternoon in the hotel as they were lying in bed.

"Sweet Bliss, they saved you, protected you, and then set you free. I would have never met you without them. I don't go to Ohio often."

"I don't ever want to go back."

"To Ohio or to The Last Riders?"

Bliss remained silent, afraid her answer would damn her. She missed The Last Riders as if a part of her had been cut off.

"You still miss them?"

Bliss nodded. "I wouldn't want to take part in the parties, though, because I wouldn't want you touching someone else, and I don't want to anymore. However, I miss how they are with each other. They're friends. I guess that's what I'm trying to say. I miss my friends."

"They were more than your friends. They were your family, and family forgives each other. That's what they do." Drake played with the tendril of hair that had been steadily growing. Since she always kept her hair so short, it had already almost grown back to normal length.

Bliss gave a shaky laugh. "Maybe in a few years. I made them pretty mad."

"I don't think you made them as mad as you believe you did."

"What do you mean?" They had been mad enough to vote her out.

"Nothing. Let's get cleaned up. It's been a long day."

Drake helped her off his lap, and then they both washed each other off.

Bliss was already half-asleep when she slid into bed, scooting over to give him plenty of room.

"Why are you all the way over there?"

Bliss opened her eyes to see him frowning at her. "I want you to be comfortable."

Drake reached out, drawing her closer until her head was lying on his shoulder. "Now I'm comfortable."

Chapter Eighteen

Drake stomped his feet on the front porch, shaking off the snow, before he reached out to knock on the door. It took several minutes for Rachel to answer, her face pale as the snow he had just kicked of his boots.

"Drake?"

"Morning, Rachel. I'm sorry to wake you up early on Christmas Eve, but I'd like to talk to Cash."

Rachel held the door wider. "Come in. He's eating breakfast." Her face turned a sickly shade of green.

"Are you all right?"

"Just morning sickness. I thought I was over it, but certain smells set it off. Watching Cash eat bacon and biscuits and gravy is more than my stomach can handle right now." She waved him toward the kitchen. "Go on in. I'm going back to bed."

"Feel better," Drake said as he went into the kitchen to find Cash with a huge plate of food in front of him.

"You eat like that every day?" Drake asked, pouring himself a cup of coffee without waiting for the offer.

Cash took another bite of his food. "It's Christmas Eve. I'll work it off this afternoon. What has you up so early? I thought you would still be in bed after last night."

Drake sat down at the kitchen table across from him. "That looks good."

"Help yourself. There's more on the stove."

Drake got up to make himself a plate, putting an extra spoonful of gravy on top of the biscuits. He then sat down, enjoying the taste of the carb-rich breakfast.

"Why were The Last Riders at the daycare center last night?" he asked after he was finished.

"How do you know we were?"

"I saw you when you left."

Cash took a sip of his coffee. "Stark likes to strike when no one's looking, so it was the only place the coward could attack."

"That explains why Stark was there, not The Last Riders."

"One of us was always keeping an eye on Bliss. Shade noticed several bikers join up with Stark the day before, so we increased the number of men watching her."

"Why care? She's not a Last Rider."

"Bliss will always be a Last Rider. Have you seen that tattoo she has?"

"I've seen it."

"You give her shit about it?"

"No, and I'm not going to. Bliss loves The Last Riders. They're the only part of her past that doesn't hurt her, other than the mistakes she made with the wives."

"Those were pretty big mistakes. That's why we had to cut her loose. She was fixated on Shade. He and Lily both tried to ignore it, but it only got worse."

"Because she felt more and more alone with each one of you marrying."

"We knew she was afraid of being alone. That's why we didn't want to have to cut her loose. But when she went after Willa, she had to be punished."

"So, you threw her out?"

"It was the worst punishment for her. She was so afraid of losing us that she was pushing us away. We figured if she lost us and learned she would still be okay, she would see she didn't have to be so afraid of being on her own anymore."

"Then Stark came back."

"Yes. We were going to take her back to the safety of the club, but Shade said you could handle it, and you did."

Drake didn't give a fuck if Shade had confidence in him or not. What he did care about was the woman sleeping in his bed.

"Bliss misses The Last Riders."

"We've never taken someone back that's been voted out. That means she would possibly have to earn the votes again, and our women are only allowed to be with The Last Riders."

"Is there any other way for her to get the votes without fucking for them?"

"She told you that?" Cash's glare showed Bliss had told him a club secret.

Drake hid the satisfaction that gave him. He didn't think Cash or the other members would be as happy with that knowledge.

"Word gets around."

"Mm-hmm," Cash said doubtfully, picking up a piece of bacon to chew on thoughtfully.

"I'll tell you this: markers can substitute for votes. No one will give Bliss markers, though. She's burned too many bridges. The men won't expect her to earn the votes again but she will have to have the votes of all the eight members and their wives. Like I said, she burned a lot of bridges.

"I could earn the markers," Drake suggested.

"To do that, you would have to become a Last Rider." Cash put the bacon down on his plate. "You want to be a Last Rider?"

"Do I have to fuck anyone but Bliss?"

"No, who you fuck is your choice."

"Do I get to fight a lot?"

"Some." Cash's lips twisted into an anticipatory smile.

"Then I'm game. It'll give me someone to ride with now that Jace is going into the service."

"It's not that easy. You haven't been asked to join. You become a prospect first—we see how you do with the other members, how you carry yourself. We don't need someone with the Porter temper running his mouth off. We keep our business to ourselves. In other words, we have to trust you and make sure you're loyal to us before we let you through the last step of the initiation, which is taking on four of the original members. Then, if you get past them and are still alive, you become one of us."

Drake stood up, carrying his dirty plate to the sink and washing it then picking up the coffee pot to refill his and Cash's cups before sitting back down. However, his affable attitude disappeared in a flash.

"Viper told me the club owed me one when the Freedom Riders wanted that land I refused to sell them, and I sold back that family property I had bought off Rachel without a profit when you came asking. Is that what you mean about markers? I think that should be enough so I don't have to do shit jobs to prove I can take you on."

He took a sip of coffee before continuing. "I don't gossip. If I did, everyone in the county would know what that back piece of land on the club's property is used for. I know how to keep a secret. Always have."

Drake stood up, staring down at Cash. "Tell Viper I want the initiation today. The land on the right of the factory is mine. When he asked to buy it, I told him no, but that I had no intention of doing anything with it other than using it for hunting. I'll sign the deed over to him when I'm a Last Rider. That should be enough for Bliss's markers. If not, I bulldoze it and put up a fucking shopping mall."

"Viper doesn't like ultimatums," Cash warned.

"My woman misses her family, and I aim to see that she gets what she wants for Christmas."

"I'll talk to him. If he says yes, who do you want to go up against?"

"You pick."

"Don't think I'll make it easy for you."

"I didn't think you would. Just don't pick Shade."

"Why? Afraid you won't win?"

"No, I don't think either of us would win, but we would both be too busted up to enjoy Christmas." Drake's lips quirked into a mocking smile.

"You're underestimating what kind of beating you're going to get. They won't hold back."

"I don't need them to." Drake slid the chair back under the table. "Don't pick yourself, either. I don't want Rachel upset, with her carrying."

Cash's lips twitched. "You think you would leave me busted up?"

"You know I love a fight just as much as you. I may have calmed down when I had Jace, but I still remember how to throw a punch."

"I'll take that into consideration when I pick who you go up against." Cash rose from the table, going to the sink. "*If* Viper agrees."

"He would be stupid not to, and Viper doesn't strike me as being anyone's fool."

"He's not. I'll go to the clubhouse and talk to him now."

Cash waited expectantly for him to leave, but Drake had one more piece of business to take care of before he left.

"Has Rachel told you what you're having yet?"

"No, she's keeping it a secret until the baby's born. Why?"

"You're having a girl. She thinks you want a boy and will be disappointed."

"She does? Rachel should know better—"

"She's from the mountains, and she's a Porter. They always want boys for firstborns."

"How do you know all this?"

Drake gave him a wry smile. "I have Porter blood, remember? I need to go." He started to walk out of the kitchen. "Call me and tell me when and where I need to be. I have a couple of things I need to take care of first. Tell Rachel Merry Christmas for me." He paused at the doorway and turned back around. "You having Christmas dinner with her brothers tomorrow?"

"I can't get out of it. If you could figure a way out of it for me, I would give both you *and* Bliss my votes," Cash joked.

Drake gave him a saccharine smile that brought a worried frown to Cash's face.

"I'll take you up on that offer. I'll keep them busy tomorrow."

"How?"

"Leave that up to me. Enjoy your Porter-free Christmas."

"Damn, this is going to be a good Christmas. I get to watch the brothers fight, *and* I don't have to share my turkey. I'm going into town to buy myself a case of beer to celebrate."

ஐ ஐ

"Dammit." Bliss set the hot cookie tray down on the counter, waving her fingers in the air to soothe the stinging pain. When it finally went away, she gingerly touched one of the cookies on the tray. It was burned to a crisp.

Dumping the entire thing into the trash, she took out another cookie tray.

"I am going to do this. I am not going to burn them this time." She didn't understand how they had burned.

After she had the dollops of dough on the cookie sheet, she went to the oven and looked at the temperature. It was what the recipe had called for. Next time, she wouldn't answer her cell phone if anyone called.

Ginny had called to wish her a Merry Christmas, and Bliss grudgingly admitted to herself she might have talked too long. She had asked Ginny to drop off the envelope containing keys to a new car for Marcus's mother. Bliss hadn't wanted her to know who the car was from, so Ginny had told her it was from a Secret Santa. Sooner or later, Marcus would outgrow believing in Santa Clause, but it wasn't going to be this year.

As she was closing the oven door with the cookie sheet inside, Bliss heard the front door slam shut.

"Drake?" she called out, not wanting to leave the cookies. It was the last of the dough. It was supposed to make over forty cookies, but twenty-nine were already in the trash.

"I'll be down in a minute. I'm going to take a shower." Drake's voice sounded muffled.

Bliss frowned. Drake typically took his shower before bed. His bedroom was downstairs, so why had he gone upstairs to the boys' bathroom? He had only gone out to get a last-minute present for Cal.

She turned on the light in the oven. Seeing the cookies were still in the little balls of uncooked dough, she figured she had enough time to go upstairs and check on him.

Bliss hurried up the steps. Maybe he had ripped open his stitches, or they were infected, and he didn't want her to know.

She opened the bathroom door, screaming at the sight of him with his shirt off.

His hands and face were a bloody mess, and his ribs were black and blue. He was washing the blood off his hands, which were swollen and resembled raw hamburger.

"What happened?" she cried out as she hastily grabbed more towels from the towel rack.

"I got in a little fight."

"On Christmas Eve? Who with? Did you call Knox? You need to go to the hospital."

Drake didn't have time to answer before Bliss heard the doorbell ring.

"Go answer the door. I'm all right," he told her.

"I'll be right back."

Bliss ran down the steps. She looked out the peephole to see who it was and thought for a second she was imagining the face staring back at her.

"Open the door, Bliss."

Shade's voice had her shaking as she did so. The Last Riders brushed by her as they filed inside one by one. After the men came in, the women each stopped to give her a hug before moving forward to let someone else take a turn.

"Looking good. I like that red sweater. May I borrow it tomorrow?" Raci grinned, giving her a tight squeeze.

It was the first Christmas she would have spent without The Last Riders, so to see them coming through the door was filling the aching emptiness that had been present all day.

"I'll think about it." Bliss bemusedly hugged the woman back.

"Where's Drake?" Rider slung an arm around her shoulder, giving her a sideways hug.

"Upstairs. He's…" Her eyes narrowed on Rider then the other men standing near. "Are you the ones who hurt Drake? Why?" She pulled angrily away from Rider.

"Don't blame us. He's the one who wanted to be a pledge and a member on the same day."

"What are you talking about, Rider?" *Drake wanted to be a Last Rider?*

"Train, go up and check on him," Viper ordered.

Bliss gasped while Train took the steps upstairs with a medic bag slung over his shoulder. The president of The Last Riders looked as bad as Drake.

"Train will patch him up good as new." Jewell gave her a warm hug. "What's burning?"

"Oh, God." Bliss ran into the kitchen, grabbing the mitt to open the oven, smoke coming from inside.

Bliss carried the cookies to the counter, practically in tears. Her Christmas Eve wasn't turning out to be the romantic occasion she had planned.

"You burned the shit out of those." Stori made a face at the charred dots that lined the black cookie sheet.

"That's the last of the dough, too. I managed to burn all forty of them." Bliss tried to shake the cookies off, but they didn't budge. Frustrated, she dumped the whole sheet in the trash.

She couldn't bring herself to move away from the trash can when she heard the doorbell again.

"I'll go answer it." Raci took off.

Bliss was willing to bet she wanted to escape the stench of the smoke still wafting around the room.

"I wanted to make cookies for Drake. I ordered dinner from King's, but I didn't want to fake baking the cookies."

"Fake baking?" Willa asked as Beth, Evie, Lily, Diamond, and Winter all crowded into the kitchen. They were dressed in church clothes. *Christmas service at the church must have just finished.* Lucky took one step into the room, his nose wrinkling at the burned smell, before turning around and going back into the living room.

"I ordered dinner from King's and pretended I cooked it," Bliss explained.

"Drake knows you can't cook." Evie went to the kitchen counter and began making coffee. "Where are the cups?"

Bliss pointed to the cabinet over the microwave, asking, "How do you know?"

"He had lunch there a couple of weeks ago, and he told King the next time you called an order in, he likes his steak medium rare."

"Why didn't he say anything?" Drake hated being lied to, yet he had known she had lied to him about cooking.

Bliss flushed at the thought of how she had accepted his compliments on her fake cooking. She was tempted to give him a fake blow job.

"I guess he didn't want to hurt your feelings."

"It's my fault for always getting someone else to take my kitchen chores. Payback is a bitch."

"That's for sure." Evie grinned. "Next time, pick a restaurant he doesn't eat at every day for lunch."

"Do you have more of the ingredients? We could help you make a batch," Willa offered, taking off her coat.

Bliss swallowed the lump in her throat. Willa wanted to help her out when, once upon a time, she wouldn't have thought about helping the woman if the roles had been reversed.

Willa caught her ashamed look, placing her hands on her hips as she glared at Bliss. "Don't you dare. This is Christmas Eve, and we're going to have fun. Got it? Now, where are the extra ingredients?"

Bliss smiled. She had definitely learned not to poke Willa's temper.

"Here." Bliss went to the cabinet to pull out more of the ingredients, and then the women went to work baking cookies.

The kitchen filled with laughter when Beth found the cookie sheet in the trash can.

"I can take care of that." Lily took it away from her sister, going to the sink.

Bliss didn't know what to say to the women as they made the cookies. It reminded her of the many Christmas Eves at the clubhouse when they would make them and spike the hot chocolate.

Lily opened the door to the oven when Bliss carried the sheet over.

"Thank you."

"You're welcome."

Bliss slid the cookies into the oven then closed the door before turning to Lily. "Lily, I don't know how to say how sorry I am."

"You already did. I'm glad you're back in the club. None of us wanted you gone."

"You didn't?" Bliss found that hard to believe. They might have forgiven her for being a bitch, but she was sure it was long after she had left the clubhouse. She looked around the room at the women skeptically. "Wait, The Last Riders are letting me back in?"

"Yes," Winter answered. "Didn't Drake tell you? He talked Viper into letting him in the club without prospecting, and he passed the initiation today. Then he used markers the club owed him to get you voted back into the club."

"That's why he was so busted up!" Bliss exclaimed, her mind going back to the men as they came through the door. He had fought Viper, Train, Rider, and Razer.

"Yes." Beth scooped more dough onto the extra cookie sheet.

"Cash said welcome back, by the way. He couldn't come tonight, since he's drunk off his ass. We dropped him off on the way here, which is why Drake got here before us." Stori turned on the light in the oven. "They're almost done."

"He was the drunkest I've ever seen him." Raci giggled as she wiped the kitchen counters. "He kept repeating, 'It's the best Christmas ever.'"

"The cookies are done." Willa handed Bliss the oven mitts, and she pulled out cookies that were the perfect color.

Setting them down on the counter, she stared at the chocolate-chip cookies that had defeated her numerous times before.

"They're perfect. Thank you."

The women all had to have one to taste-test the batch. Then Bliss slid the tray Beth had prepared into the oven.

Drake and the rest of the men came in as the last batch was baking. She gave Drake worried glances, but she was relieved when he gave her a reassuring smile, grabbing several cookies for himself when Rider, Shade, and Train began devouring them.

"You don't want any, Viper?" Bliss felt awkward around the leader, still finding it hard to believe she had been accepted back in the club.

"No, thanks." Viper winced when he tried to offer a smile. "My jaw is too sore."

"Poor baby," Winter crooned with mock sympathy. "I've told you that you should find a better way to vote in members."

"Nothing else would be as much fun."

"I don't know about that. The way we vote in the women is pretty damn fun for me."

"Rider, if you want to vote in men the way we vote in women, go for it."

As Rider took another cookie and moved away, the women all burst out laughing.

Razer and Train both looked like Drake hadn't been any easier on them. They reminded her of the night they had gotten in a fight with the Destructors at the Pink Slipper, but it had taken several of the bikers to give them the beating Drake had. She wondered how Rider had managed to get through the fight seemingly without a mark on him.

Evie had called King and asked him to increase Bliss's order substantially. When it arrived, it reminded Bliss of old times, when they sat around the kitchen and tried to grab the food before it was gone then sat and talked until late in the night.

Drake leaned back, placing his arm around Bliss's waist. "Having fun?"

Bliss leaned tiredly against him, yawning. "It's the best Christmas Eve I've ever had. Thank you. I'll always remember it."

"I will, too." Drake winced, trying to shift her to a more comfortable position.

"I'm sorry." Bliss started to straighten off him, but he tugged her back.

"Stay still. You're not the only one who's going to remember this night."

"Can I ask you a question?" When he nodded, she asked, "Why does Rider look so good? I would have never known he was in the fight if Winter hadn't told me."

"Damned if I know. I gave him some of my best punches. That man has an iron jaw. He should look worse than any of us. The only reason I got past him was because I lasted so long against him."

"Even when Jared shot him, it only took him a couple of days to recover." Train spoke up from the chair across the table. "He's a freak of nature. Do you know how he got his nickname in the service?" He waited for Drake to raise his brows in question. "When we were in the service, we woke up to enemy fire. We were all scared shitless, running around in the dark, trying to wake up and return fire. Thank God Shade had come in that night from a mission and was still awake. He gave us enough time to retaliate.

"We were so freaked out we didn't notice Rider had been shot until it was over and were assessing the damage. Ten men never made it out of their bunk rolls that night. Rider coded on me twice, and when I was about to give up, I got him back. They flew him out, and once I managed to hitch a ride with the next helicopter two hours later, I went to the hospital to find him. It took me thirty minutes to find him in the X-ray room, fucking the technician. He was fucking her from behind as if he didn't have three bullets in him."

Drake held his ribs. "Which was why you called him Rider, for 'ride her,' right?"

"Yep." Train laughed. "He gave her the ride of her life after being declared dead twice."

"Too bad I don't remember it. I was too full of painkillers and the pot Shade had packed in to us the night before."

"Want me to call Tate to bring you something to take the edge off the pain?" Bliss offered noticing Drake's pale complexion.

"No, thanks. He wouldn't bring it, anyway. Tate, Greer, and Dustin aren't talking to me right now."

"Why not?" The cousins seemed too tight to not be on speaking terms.

"I told them Cash helped me become a member, and they're so mad at me they aren't talking to me or him. They even told him they aren't coming to Christmas dinner."

Bliss wondered about the triumphant smile on his broken face, but she figured he didn't believe the brothers would stay mad long.

"Is Cash upset?"

"Yeah, he's all broken up about it."

Bliss realized then Drake was joking. No man who was upset his brothers-in-law wouldn't be coming Christmas day would be singing "best Christmas ever."

"Is Rachel mad?"

"At me, not Cash. I told him she's having a girl. When he told her I had told him, she was so mad she wouldn't even call to cuss me out. She's not talking to me, either."

"Thank God the craziness that runs in that family missed you."

"What makes you think that?"

Bliss stopped smiling. "It did, didn't it?" The Porter brothers were constantly in fights. Plus, Rachel had special gifts, and it was rumored her brothers did, too…

"I've been known to do some crazy shit in my life."

"What's the craziest thing you've done?" Bliss quirked her head to the side, studying his face up close.

"The craziest?" He stopped to think about it. "When Stephanie cheated on me, I kind of went crazy and started cage fighting on the weekends when she had visitation. It kept me from wanting to beat the shit out of the bastard she moved in with when I kicked her out."

"You were a cage fighter?" Viper groaned. "Does Cash know?"

"Hell no. No one knew. Stephanie would have used it to try to get custody away from me."

"That would have been useful knowledge *before* the fight." Viper turned to Shade, who was sitting at the table with Lily on his lap. "That was never part of the information you gave me on Drake when I told you to check him out."

"It's Christmas Eve. The info was coming in slow."

"Exactly when did you find out that piece of information?" Viper's eyes narrowed on his enforcer.

"Right about the time it was your turn. I was going to tell you, but Winter told me not to."

Viper glared at his innocent-looking wife. "Why in the hell not?"

"You're constantly telling me how fighting makes you horny. I still remember the last time you were in a fight. If you think I was going to deny myself another night like that, you're as crazy as Greer."

Lily rose reluctantly from Shade's lap. "We need to get home. Ember is babysitting John and Beth's twins for us."

The others also stood to leave, going into the living room to say their good-byes. Bliss stood back as the men all talked in the doorway and the women put on their coats.

"You happy?"

Bliss gazed at Shade. It no longer hurt to look at him.

"You were right." All the times she had begged for his attention, he had told her he wasn't the one for her.

"About what?" Shade paused at putting on his leather gloves.

"That I didn't love you. That being in love wasn't about making yourself happy, but the one you loved. I couldn't understand that until Drake. He works hard at making me happy. I'm not an easy woman to love, though. It would be hard for me, but I would let him go if I thought it would make him happier. It would break me, but I would let him go."

"Do you know how Drake managed to get custody of Jace during a time when it wasn't easy for a man to, especially one in Treepoint?"

She shrugged. "I just assumed because Stephanie was the one who left."

"No, it was because Drake never lets go of anything that's his. It's a Porter trait, like how Greer's still driving his father's old truck. Drake told Stephanie if she didn't sign custody over to him, she wouldn't live to raise him anyway. He's kept his family's property intact for years, despite big money being offered for it from the lumber companies. He even bought Rachel's, despite the mortgage crisis going on that had him losing his ass from not selling. He saved it for her until she could buy it back someday, which Cash did. He managed to save his company by working his ass off, keeping a roof over his and Jace's head by cage fighting every weekend."

Shade finished putting his gloves on. "You don't have to worry about Drake ever leaving you. When I went into his office to try to convince him to sell the property next to the factory, he asked me if it was true that the women were only allowed to be with The Last Riders. I told him yes, and he asked to join the club. I told him no."

"When was this?" Had Drake been interested in her enough to join The Last Riders before they had told her to leave?

Bliss's heart felt as if she was standing in front of a roaring fire, melting any lingering doubts that Drake would wake up one day and no longer want her in his life. Trying to join The Last Riders was the type of gesture Shade would have done for Lily.

"The day before we voted you out. Merry Christmas, Bliss."

"Merry Christmas, Shade."

Bliss watched the motorcycles pull out of the driveway from the window, holding the curtain back. She noticed the snow begin to fall.

A warm arm circled her waist from behind.

"Wish you were going with them?"

"No. Actually, I was thinking I'm glad I'm not out in the cold, freezing my ass off." Bliss dropped the curtain, turning into his arms. "Thank you for giving me my friends back."

"You never lost them, Bliss. They've been watching over you. They were there the night Stark attacked. If my cousins hadn't been there, Stark still wouldn't have succeeded. The Last Riders would have stopped them."

"I know. I saw them when I was running across the parking lot."

"And you still didn't call out for them?"

"No, I didn't need to. I knew you would be there. I trusted you."

"You just gave me the best Christmas present I could have asked for."

"Then I guess I should take back that new motorcycle I had Stud custom-make for you that I hid in the back of my garage."

Drake stared down at her in astonishment. "You bought me one of Stud's bikes? I was going to buy Jace and Cal each one for a graduation presents, but he said he had two years of pre-orders."

"He did. He's running behind schedule."

"How did you convince him?"

"I didn't. Sex Piston did. I talked to her when she tried to fix my hair. I told her if she could convince Stud to sell me three bikes, I'd convince Jace to sell back their car. Fat Louise sold it to Crazy Bitch when she bought a new car. Crazy Bitch got aggravated at it when it kept breaking and sold it without telling the other bitches. They've been mad at her ever since."

"Three?"

Bliss nodded. "One for you, Jace, and Cal. Three men in Kentucky aren't very happy with me right now for swiping their Christmas gifts."

"I know three who are going to be ecstatic, but I think you might have trouble convincing the boys to give up that car. They've grown attached to it. I told you it's a classic."

"Yeah, it's a classic. It's sitting at Jo's repair shop right now. The front passenger seat went through the floorboard. Jace sold it to me for fifty dollars two days ago."

"Fifty dollars? He gave Crazy Bitch a thousand for it."

"Lesson learned: never buy a car off a woman named Crazy Bitch."

Chapter Nineteen

"One, don't make me come. Two, don't make me come. Three—"

"Will you stop doing that?" Drake stopped sucking on the pebbled nipple long enough to raise himself on his arms and stare down at the woman wiggling on the dick he was thrusting inside her wet pussy. He was sore as hell from the fights the night before; he kept telling himself it was mind over matter when each thrust sent pain screaming through his body. The only thing that mattered was his aching dick. Bliss could get a rise from a man at death's door.

"Then don't make me come!" she panted. Her hands that had been gripping the sides of her pillow went to his chest, her thumbs playing with his nipples. The ring he had placed on her finger when they had gone to bed the night before flashed when the light from the bedside lamp hit the large, sparkling diamond.

Drake raised himself up higher, wanting to see the glide of his slick dick going in and out of the pussy stretched wide to take him.

"Don't do that! It makes me want to come when you watch us fuck."

Drake didn't lift his eyes, holding back his climax. Each stroke dragged his cock across her clit, making her wetter for him.

His hand went down to her stomach, pressing down as he thrust upward. Her loud screams let him know he had rubbed the spot he was aiming for. Her pussy clenched then began a series of spasms that had his cock filling her as each thrust knocked the headboard against the wall.

He lowered his seriously aching body onto hers when he finished, watching every second of her climax.

"You're going to have to come quieter from now on. Jace and Cal will be able to hear you from all the way upstairs in their bedrooms if you don't."

Bliss slid her arms around Drake until she could grip an ass cheek in both of her hands. "I told you I won't move in until Jace leaves to join the service. I'm not going to have the gossips in town saying anything to hurt him."

"That's why you haven't moved in?"

She had cared enough about the boys not to want them to think badly of her. Behind the naughty exterior Bliss projected to the town, Drake knew she was sensitive to what others thought about her; she had just learned to hide it, even from herself.

Bliss began massaging his ass cheeks, and Drake pulled out of her before she could get him hard again. He didn't have time to fuck her again before Jace and Cal returned home to open their Christmas presents.

"Your ex-wife saw me at the grocery store and told me that everyone in school was teasing him about his dad's hot girlfriend."

"Why didn't you tell me?"

"Because, at one time, it was something I would have done myself. I figured I deserved it. Payback's a bitch."

"The only bitch was Stephanie for acting that way." He made a mental note to call her the following day. When he finished with her, she would run across the street when she saw Bliss.

Drake let her doze back to sleep while he showered and shaved. He then tossed the covers off Bliss when he came out of the bathroom.

"Time to get up. Jace and Cal will be here any minute. It's Christmas morning, so he won't knock before coming in. Then he'll see just how hot his soon-to-be stepmother really is," Drake threatened.

Bliss squealed, jumping out of bed. The only thing Drake saw was a flash, and then she was gone, the bathroom door closing behind her.

"I was only teasing," he called out, getting dressed and listening to her mumbling threats. "You're not going to do anything," Drake yelled back at her mumbling. "My dick is why you fell in love with me."

"No, it isn't. I fell in love with the way you fuck me," she said, the bathroom door still firmly closed, the shower running.

"It's the same thing."

"No, it isn't. That's like saying, 'which came first: the chicken or the egg.'"

"I'm never going to understand that logic." Drake sat on the side of the bed, tugging on his boots. He was going to be prepared to ride when they went to see the motorcycle she had bought him for Christmas. Damn, he had wanted to make the holiday special for Bliss, and she had almost outdone him on presents. She thought she was wearing his gift to her when the best one was going to be there any second.

"Bliss, hurry."

She came out dripping wet, giving him a fuming glare. "I would have already been dressed if you hadn't dragged me back to bed after my first shower."

Drake laughed. "I told you I had a special present for you."

"You gave me several presents last night. They were all special." She put an extra bounce into her ass as she wiggled into her jeans.

"I'll go make us some hot chocolate. Don't take long."

"I'm almost ready. Don't forget the marshmallows."

"I won't. I bought extra."

ꕥ

Bliss stared after Drake, wondering about the cryptic comment. Then the doorbell rang as she was choosing a green sweater to wear with her black jeans. She put on a pair of warm boots, wanting to be prepared to ride when she took the men to see their new bikes. Opening the bedroom door, she hurried out to see Jace and Cal.

She turned the corner of the hallway, coming to a stop when she saw the Christmas tree. Santa had come the night before, and he hadn't forgotten her that year. At least a dozen presents that hadn't been there before were shoved under the bulging tree. He seemed to have made up for every year he had missed with her.

On the chair beside the Christmas tree was a cream-colored coat with fur cuffs and a fur hood, carefully arranged with a red bow. Next to the coat was a little girl dressed in a red velvet dress with a tiny red ribbon dangling from her hair. Her feet were in shiny black shoes that were swinging back and forth.

"Darcy!" Bliss couldn't hold back her sobs as she ran into the room.

The little girl excitedly jumped up and ran to her, holding out her arms. Bliss reached down, lifting the slight bundle into her arms.

"I thought you couldn't get the court date approved until after Christmas?" Bliss looked at Cal who was standing next to Jace and Drake. His eyes were brimming with tears.

"Drake hired Diamond to push it through for me. They gave me custody of her yesterday. She's mine now." His hand tightened on the yellow envelope in his hand before he reached out to hand it to her.

Bliss shifted Darcy to her hip as she opened the large envelope. She stared down uncomprehendingly as she flipped through and read the official papers.

"The first one is my dad's legal document giving up his parental rights. The second one is my custody papers, giving me legal custody of Darcy." Cal's voice broke, but he continued. "The third paper is me giving up Darcy for adoption to you and Drake. The fourth one is giving you and Drake permission to care for her and the medical releases while I'm in the service until the adoption goes through. If you want her, she's yours."

Bliss buried her face in Darcy's sweet smelling hair. "I want her more than anything I've ever wanted in my life." She felt the little girl's arms circle her neck as she laid her head on her shoulder.

Bliss carried her to Cal, who was manfully trying not to cry. "Are you sure?"

"I can't offer her what you and Drake can. I can't give her the forever home she needs. I wish I could, but I can't. It's not fair to make her wait."

She turned to her fiancé. "Are you sure, Drake? We never talked about children." She held her breath, waiting for his answer. *Please, God, just this once, don't let the happiness slip through my grasp.*

"I knew I wasn't capable of raising Darcy by myself, or I would have taken her when she went into foster care. I don't know a thing about raising little girls. I thought you could help me with that part." He wrapped his arms around both of them. "I'm going to enjoy having two pretty girls to come home to."

Darcy raised her head from Bliss's shoulder. "Did you get what you wanted for Christmas?"

"Yes, Darcy, I did." Bliss placed a gentle kiss on her cheek. "Did you?"

"Yes. Bubby told me I'm going to stay with you and Drake." Bliss laughed when Darcy reached out to pat Drake's cheek.

"Is that okay with you?"

The girl nodded happily then frowned. "You won't try to take my blanket away?" Darcy clutched it to her tightly.

"No," Bliss reassured her through her tears of happiness.

"Then it's okay. All the kids at school are going to want to come home with you, too, but I'm going to tell them you're all mine."

"You're going to share her with me, aren't you, Darcy?" Drake asked with mock worry.

"I can share with you, not them. She's going to be my mama, not theirs."

"No, I won't be theirs." Bliss's voice wobbled. "Do you want to open our presents now?" Bliss had wrapped Darcy's presents the day before. Cal was supposed to have taken them to her at her foster home after dinner. The men had planned the Christmas surprise so she could see Darcy open her presents.

The little girl clapped as Cal and Jace pulled out the presents for her to open.

"It wasn't easy, but I managed to get everything on your Christmas list."

Bliss looked away from Darcy ripping open her presents to Drake. "I didn't make a list…"

Drake pulled out a colored piece of construction paper that had been folded and unfolded numerous times. "I sneaked it off the wall where it was pinned at the daycare."

Bliss stared at the numerous pictures she had glued down: the home with a family smiling around the Christmas tree, opening presents; a large home with the Christmas lights shining; a cream-colored coat a pretty model was wearing as she shopped; a diamond ring; and a Christmas dinner on a large table surrounded by people.

"I think you missed one thing."

"What?" Drake frowned, looking down at the picture.

"The Christmas dinner. I hope you're not expecting me to cook it. If I did, it wouldn't look like that," Bliss warned.

"King is having it delivered this afternoon."

Bliss laughed, pulling him to her. "Then I agree with Cash. This is the best Christmas ever."

Epilogue

Drake leaned against his car, staring down at his watch and sighing impatiently.

She was late again. He fondly remembered the days when he used to text her and she came running. Now he was lucky to get a text that would tell him she was coming.

He knew she was approaching when he saw the men across the street come to a stop, gazing appreciatively at the woman walking down the street. A smile came to his lips when he saw his ladies holding hands. The little girl skipping happily next to his woman was talking animatedly as they neared.

Bliss was wearing the thick coat he had given her three winters ago. With her black boots, she looked sexy as hell. As he watched, Bliss reached up, brushing back her hair that the wind had sent blowing, giving her a sexy, tousled, I-just-got-out-of-bed look. It reached to below her chin, brushing her shoulders. If he had thought Bliss was eye-catching when she had short hair, with longer hair, she looked like a sex kitten.

The men who were staring at her looked away in disappointment when the diamond ring she wore flashed in the winter sun.

Bliss thought he had given her a big diamond to make her happy. She was wrong. He had given it to her to make him happy. He wanted any man who looked at her to know she was taken.

"What time will they be home, Mommy?"

"I don't know. They'll call when their plane lands." Bliss's voice was soft and happy.

Drake smiled. His daughter was anxious for her brother and stepbrother to be home.

"Daddy, do you know…?"

"You heard your mother. They're going to call."

"But it's Christmas Eve. They promised they would be here yesterday. What if they don't make it for Christmas?"

"They'll make it. Cal and Jace both promised. Their plane was delayed. As soon as they can, they'll be here. They don't want to miss you opening your presents in the morning."

"I won't open them until they get here," Darcy promised fervently as her father opened the car door for her to climb inside. Drake watched patiently as she buckled herself into her booster seat before closing the door.

After opening Bliss's door, he took the packages from her hand, giving her a kiss that stamped his ownership over her for the remaining men who hadn't moved on.

"Wow! What was that for?" Bliss grinned up at him.

"This morning…and at that asshole standing in front of the diner, whom I'm about to give a black eye."

Her gaze went over the roof of the car to see who he was threatening.

"Oh, that's just Silas, Ginny's brother." Bliss gave him a friendly wave.

"I know who he is. Get in the car."

Bliss got inside the car, smiling. Then Drake went around the front of the car, giving Silas a glare that sent him on his way.

"That wasn't nice," Bliss said when he got inside.

"He was being a jackass."

"Daddy, who was being a jackass?"

"See what you did." Bliss snickered. "No one, Darcy. Daddy's just in a grumpy mood."

"Oh." The little girl happily began swinging her feet.

"We'll drop the packages off at home and get dressed for the party at the church tonight. All your cousins are going to be there." Bliss chatted as they pulled out into the traffic.

"Is Logan going to be there?"

Bliss shot Drake a glance. Both of them knew what was coming.

"Yes," Drake answered.

"I don't want to go. I'll stay home and wait for Cal and Jace."

"You have to go. You're not old enough to stay home by yourself."

"Logan's mean to me. He says I'm not a Porter."

Drake grinned. His cousins still threw the same insult at him. The difference was Darcy really wasn't, and the sensitive girl took it to heart when the boy made the claim.

"Just ignore him," Drake advised. "That's what I do."

Darcy went silent, staring morosely out the window.

Drake pulled into the driveway and ushered Bliss and Darcy inside.

"What's the rush?"

"If we don't get there early enough, the turkey will be all gone. Between all The Last Riders and the Porters, it's already slim pickings."

"There will be plenty of food. Rachel made an extra turkey, and Willa made an extra ham."

"Cal and Jace will probably be there before it's over."

"We better hurry, then, because once those boys start eating, nothing will be left." With that, Bliss ran up the steps. The sight almost had him agreeing with Darcy about staying home.

Darcy followed her mother upstairs more slowly, sending him a pleading look over her shoulder. Drake gave her an encouraging smile.

"I'll make sure Logan behaves."

"Okay."

Drake took his time getting dressed, knowing he would be ready well before his women. He wasn't wrong. It took them a good hour longer than him before they were heading to Lucky's church.

Darcy's reservations about coming disappeared when John, Chance, Noah, and little Maggie came running to greet her. The children disappeared into the crowd. Drake didn't worry, though. Each adult in the room would keep an eye on the children.

"I'm going to go help set the food up." Bliss rose up on her toes to brush a kiss on his lips.

"Don't be gone long."

"I won't," she promised, giving him a bright smile before braving the huge crowd.

Drake found the punch bowl already surrounded by The Last Riders. He didn't have to ask Rider if it was spiked since a smaller bowl had been set up at another table with Rachel pouring cups for the children.

He took a cup from Viper.

"Careful with that," he warned. "Rider and Train made it this year."

Drake took a small sip, nearly gagging. It was more liquor than fruit. At least the huge table of food should help with keeping the men relatively sober, if not from puking up the horrible concoction the two had made.

Shade caught his reaction. "It's better than last year when Penni made it."

"Or the year before when Greer did. The women didn't even talk to any of us Christmas Day. That son of a bitch was responsible for all of us having to walk home in the freezing cold after the women left with the children," Cash needlessly reminded them.

Drake had been one of them walking home. He had woken up the next morning with the worst hangover in history. He had waited for Bliss and Darcy to open their presents before driving to Greer's house and beating the shit out of him. Drake was sure it was one Christmas present he would never forget.

"I'm going to tell my daddy!" Darcy's tearful voice had Drake turning to seeing Logan standing next to his daughter. Her pretty green dress was drenched in punch. Darcy was holding an empty cup, the contents of which Drake assumed Logan had forced her to spill on herself.

Rachel had turned around to talk to Holly when she saw Darcy. She immediately began trying to wipe off her dress.

Drake was about to step forward when Greer came barreling toward his nephew, slapping him up against the back of his head.

"What's wrong with you, boy? Porters never make a woman cry!"

Holly opened her mouth but snapped it closed when Greer shot her a do-not-interfere look.

Logan turned bright red from being the focus of so many adult stares.

"I couldn't let her drink it, Uncle Greer."

"Why not?" Holly asked before Greer could.

"Because Chance had switched that cup with one from the other table when no one was looking."

The room went silent. The men went pale, and Razer went for Chance. Drake almost felt sorry for the young boy.

Chance and Noah were going through a mischievous phase, pulling jokes on each other when the opportunity was available.

"I'm sorry, Dad. I meant it for Noah."

"Chance, you can spend the rest of the night by yourself in the corner, watching everyone else have fun."

"I'm sorry, Dad." Razer didn't try to hide his disappointment in his son's actions.

"Go, and don't think that will be your only punishment. When Noah is unwrapping his Christmas presents in the morning, you will be writing letters of apology to both Darcy and her parents."

"Yes, sir." The dejected boy went to the corner where his furious mother had a chair waiting for him.

"That's the last time you men get your own punch." Winter picked up the big bowl, taking it into the church kitchen.

The men all glared at the boy while Drake burst out laughing, slapping Razer on the back.

"Don't be too mad at him. He did us all a favor. That's the worst punch we've had yet."

The atmosphere lightened.

Greer ruffled Logan's hair. "That's the way you watch out for your cousin."

Logan's hand went to his hair to straighten it and he cast a shy glance at Darcy. "She's not my cousin! We're not kin."

Darcy's face filled with hurt and she started to turn to Bliss, who had come to see what was going on with her daughter. From her expression, Drake could tell another boy was about to be sent to the corner with his tail tucked between his legs.

"I brought you something, Darcy." Logan reached into his pocket, pulling out a small wooden figurine. "I made it myself. Daddy taught me to whittle, and I know you want a kitten, but you can't have one since you're allergic." He tentatively held out his gift in the palm of his hand.

Drake held back his gasp while most of the women couldn't. The beautiful wooden figurine was a work of infinite patience and skill. It was a curled-up small kitten, sleeping. It had been buffed until it shone.

Darcy gave Logan a timid smile, reaching out to take her special gift.

"Thank you."

"You're welcome."

The children gathered around to see for themselves, complimenting Logan on his skill.

Bliss slipped an arm around Drake's waist, leaning against him, and Drake placed an arm around her shoulder, tugging her closer.

"I think we're in trouble," she teased, nodding at Logan who was trying to manfully shrug off the many compliments while gazing at Darcy with puppy dog eyes.

"I wonder if Winter already threw out that punch."

Drake winced when his wife shoved an elbow into his stomach.

"You need anything?" Drake asked, trying to make amends for his lame joke.

"Yes, hold me tighter."

It never failed to pierce his soul when she would ask that of him. He wondered if she would ever feel the security of his love. Each time she asked him to hold her tighter, it was as if she were assuring herself he was still there.

"Why are you looking so sad?" Bliss asked, staring up at him.

Drake pulled her even more tightly against him. "Nothing, sweet Bliss." He looked across the room before telling her, "Look over at the door."

Jace and Cal had both just entered.

Bliss squealed in joy, taking off, whereas Drake waited patiently for his sons to make their way to him through the well-wishers.

"Dad." Both Jace and Cal reached out to give him a bear hug.

"About time you boys got your asses here. Your mom and sister have been driving me crazy."

"We hitched a ride with Santa." Cal laughed, reaching down to pick up his sister and giving her a noisy kiss on her cheek.

"Bubby! I knew you would make it!"

"So did I!" Bliss joined in. "I new Santa wouldn't disappoint me. All I wanted for Christmas was all of my family at home."

Drake bent down to whisper in her ear, "You must have been a good girl this year."

She wrapped her arms around his shoulders, hugging him tightly. "Santa will never forget which door our family is behind. We're going to be there forever."

Drake returned her hug. Bliss had just given him her greatest gift. It was a Christmas miracle worth waiting for—faith in their love.

"Ew...Mommy and Daddy are kissing again," Darcy complained.

Bliss broke away, gasping. "Daddy was just wishing me a Merry Christmas."

Jace, Cal, and Darcy moved to the food table. When they were out of earshot, Drake grabbed Bliss back.

"Daddy will be wishing you a *very* Merry Christmas when we get home and everyone is asleep."

Bliss giggled. "One, you can try to make me come. Two, I'm going to make you come first. Three...after we put together Darcy's new bike."

"Santa's going to be coming tonight. Jace and Cal can put the bike together. That's what elves are for."

~Merry Christmas~

Books By Jamie Begley:

The Last Riders Series:

Razer's Ride

Viper's Run

Knox's Stand

Shade's Fall

Cash's Fight

Shade

Lucky's Choice

Biker Bitches Series:

Sex Piston

Fat Louise

Merry Blissmas

The VIP Room Series:

Teased

Tainted

King

Predators MC Series:

Riot

Stand Off

Porter Brothers Trilogy:

Keeping What's His

The Dark Souls Series:

Soul Of A Man

Soul Of A Woman

About the Author

"I was born in a small town in Kentucky. My family began poor, but worked their way to owning a restaurant. My mother was one of the best cooks I have ever known, and she instilled in all her children the value of hard work, and education.

Taking after my mother, I've always love to cook, and became pretty good if I do say so myself. I love to experiment and my unfortunate family has suffered through many. They now have learned to steer clear of those dishes. I absolutely love the holidays and my family puts up with my zany decorations.

For now, my days are spent writing, writing, and writing. I have two children who both graduated this year from college. My daughter does my book covers, and my son just tries not to blush when someone asks him about my books.

Currently I am writing four series of books- The Last Riders, The Dark Souls, The VIP Room, and Biker Bitches series.

All my books are written for one purpose- the enjoyment others fi nd in them, and the expectations of my fans that inspire me to give it my best. In the near future I hope to take a weekend break and visit Vegas that will hopefully be this summer. Right now I am typing away on my next story and looking forward to traveling this summer!"

Jamie loves receiving emails from her fans,
JamieBegley@ymail.com

Find Jamie here,
https://www.facebook.com/AuthorJamieBegley

Get the latest scoop at Jamie's official website,
JamieBegley.net

75567446R00117

Made in the USA
Columbia, SC
19 August 2017